A KID UNDER THE TWO WOLVES - PART I

JOSEPH GEORGE

Copyright © Joseph George
All Rights Reserved.

This book has been published with all efforts taken to make the material error-free after the consent of the author. However, the author and the publisher do not assume and hereby disclaim any liability to any party for any loss, damage, or disruption caused by errors or omissions, whether such errors or omissions result from negligence, accident, or any other cause.

While every effort has been made to avoid any mistake or omission, this publication is being sold on the condition and understanding that neither the author nor the publishers or printers would be liable in any manner to any person by reason of any mistake or omission in this publication or for any action taken or omitted to be taken or advice rendered or accepted on the basis of this work. For any defect in printing or binding the publishers will be liable only to replace the defective copy by another copy of this work then available.

Contents

CHAPTER ONE

It was a good evening.

The children in the class were very happy, and their voices could be heard all around. Their smiling faces and speech are just signs of welcoming so many happy days ahead.

Today was a much happier day for them than usual because they have vacation days from tomorrow. Everyone's face was full of joy, and it also had no boundaries.

The whole classroom was a hotbed of unforgettable memories of the days to come. The memories of the days to come were beyond their comprehension, but they are trying to convey that to each other.

As a barrier, although the teachers would occasionally ask the children to keep quiet, none of the teachers' taboos can set limits to their happiness. So, soon the children will start talking without realizing it.

But only one child in the class is looking out through the window, not wanting to talk to anyone anymore. He was a very handsome little boy, his name is "John".

His eyes are fixed on the window in the classroom and John was not ready to take his eye off, because looking out through the window, he could see the big school gate, and he was also waiting for his mummy's car to arrive near that big school gate.

Occasionally John's attention is intertwined with the voice of the children in the classroom because most of the events they say and experiences are just experiences and contexts that are going to happen and have happened in his life.

John is now looking forward to the arrival of his mummy rather than the good experience that is going to happen next. Mummy was the only thing on his mind because John loved his mummy so much.

Now mummy is the only one in his mind, "sweet mummy coming to pick me up"

But daddy rarely comes to school to take him home when daddy comes, it will be a surprise to him but anyway, now John is well aware that he is now likely to be his mummy because John is very busy going to see daddy tomorrow.

Daddy works in a faraway place and even if he asked to take him there, he does not agree.

"My sweet daddy, I miss you so......"

"Hey John....."

John turned around when he heard someone calling behind him, it was his friend Allen.

"Hai Allen" John also answered.

Allen came close to John and started talking to John about something,

"Hey John, what are your plans for vacation?"

While hearing this question a smile appeared on John's face, and he tried to say something, but he didn't know what to say because he was so happy.

"That,... I know,... We... We are going to daddy's house to see daddy this vacation and mummy says there's daddy and daddy's daddy, so we will go to many places...."

It wasn't either long before John began to walk into the memories holding Allen's hand, it began to get too far now.

"Okay Allen, where are you going this vacation?"

Allen began to speak with a slight sigh, "Never,... I am not going anywhere because my grandmother was admitted to hospital and my mom told me that this leave couldn't go anywhere."

Seeing Allen in a terrible condition, John was disturbed and the smile on John's face suddenly faded.

"Oops, Don't worry Allen.... "I will bring lots of chocolates and toys for you when I'll be back as I have brought for you before."

Allen looked at John with a smile.

John continued, "My mummy and my daddy love you so much, and they will buy whatever you ask for."

"Thanks John,..." Allen said with a smile and stopped.

After a moment of silence, John asked Allen again a question, "Allen,... Do you know Donna?"

Allen continued slowly with a smile, "Hey John, how many times have you been asking the same question?"

John got a shock, that's when John realized that the same question he had asked Allen many times.

"Oh,... Oh,...sorry Allen,..., I forgot...."

"It is okay John, let me ask you a question? why,... Do you love Donna?"

John could not say anything in response because he was full of shame.

"Allen,... Because,...l, ...sorry"

Allen continued, looking into John's eyes again, "John, do you love Donna more than your mummy....?"

Hearing this, John's eyes slid away from Allen and fell down.

John still could not say anything. However John Whispered, "No,... I don't know."

John and Allen heard the sound of the gate being pulled open, suddenly their eyes darted out the window.

When the gate opened, John realized that it was the mummy's car, but he did not have time to think about anything.

"Yes mummy came..."

John immediately grabbed the bag in front of him and kissed Allen and ran out.

All the children in the class quickly turned their attention to John, who ran away, but John's attention was only on his mummy.

Soon the teachers tried to stop him, but John adventurously escaped them all. He came down the stairs, but John's run slowed down and came to a scene as if to cry because the gate in front of him was closed. John raised his head and looked helplessly at the big gate.

John's eyes filled with tears and remembered the mummy outside the gate,and realized that nothing could be done.

John turned around when he heard someone walking behind him, 'It was the school warden.'

A fear passed through his eyes. How can children not be afraid to see his horny mustache, Black plump body, and bald head,...?

The school warden was walking closer to him, John put his foot back, his legs were shaking, and eyes were full too.

However, John refused to be afraid to look at the school warden, John immediately gathered his courage and began to walk towards the school warden.

At first, John walked slowly and then ran over to the school warden.

John approaches the school warden and placed his rough hand on his chest and told him horseradish eyes, "Please, can you open this gate because I want to see my mummy,...."

But this time John was shocked because of a smile on the face of the school warden who scares the children.

The school Warden patted John on the cute cheek with a smile and said," I will open it,...Aren't you happy,....?"

John wiped away the tears when he heard these words and said, "thanks" with a smile.

The two walked forward.

The school warden was in front and behind John. While walking the school warden tried to talk to John.

"You will no longer see me here when you return to school after your vacation, I am retiring from work here and going home to my daughter's hometown, then you cannot see me,... I can't either."

The school Warden continued, "I cannot think of leaving you."

But John did not answer because his whole attention was on the gate key, John just nodded slowly.

"John, are you coming to my daughter's house with me?"

But this time John gave no particular answer and only gave a smile, 'That was a very cute smile' because now the gate is open.

John did not have time to think of anything else, he ran to his mummy without looking behind.

John saw the mummy standing near the car, when she saw John a smile appeared on his mummy's face.

John ran over and quickly leaned Closer to the mummy and hugged his sweet mummy.

"Mummy, why didn't you come near the school gate to pick me up? "

Mummy must have liked John's question with his eyes full and mummy said as she bent down and gave John a smirk on his lips.

"Sweetie,...I was waiting outside for you because school is not over yet. Anyway,... I'm so sorry baby,..."

"It's okay," John said with a smile.

Quickly both's attention turns to the horrible sound heard from behind.

By then all the children who had left the school rushed through the gate to the outside, Allen also was in that group.

"Allen" John Whispered.

Seeing Allen, John quickly passed the mummy and ran closer to Allen.

"John, let me give you a gift..? Your favorite gift."

Allen took a gift of something from the bag and showed it to John. 'It was a colorful paper plane.'

"Wow, amazing" John looked into Allen's Eyes.

John and Allen would make many paper planes like this when they were alone in the class.

This is their favorite pastime, but only Allen knows how to make a paper plane well, so it is common for Allen to make and give it to John.

"John, you'll have to take this with you wherever you go, so you can remember me."

While saying this Allen's eyes fell on the school bus which was about to leave.

Allen quickly kissed John and ran towards the bus.

"Bye, ...John..."

"Bye,... Bye Allen,...Sure I will see you again,..... Bye..." John said loudly.

John used to go home on the school bus with Allen, but today he cannot, because his mummy came to pick him up.

If he could, John had something important to say to Allen. The sadness of not being able to say it is well on John's mind.

Suddenly John turned back as if he remembered something and looked inside the car, Mummy was still there.

John went to his mummy without concentrating on anything and also didn't forget to take special care not to miss the paper plane and kept it safe in his bag.

"I will keep this until I see Allen again, then Allen will be happy. John told himself.

John got near the car without delay. Mummy did not ask John anything about what had happened because he was sure that mummy had seen everything that had happened.

"Mummy, do you know how hard I worked to get out of the school?"

"Why," mummy asked.

" I was released only because I cried and told the school warden."

"Oh,... Was that it...? I realized that earlier too..."

Mummy again kissed John on his forehead who stood out of her door window.

"Okay, baby come on, and take your seat" mummy's soft voice hit John in his ear.

"Yes mummy, sure ", he went to the seat on mummy's right side, and as usual mummy made sure his door was closed.

Mummy is always like this, it will show on the car screen even if no car door is closed, but mummy always starts the journey only after making sure that his door is closed.

John carefully monitors the mummy's every move and then John remembered an important thing," Tiffin box,....."

Suddenly John searched for the tiffin box from inside the bag and by then Mummy had started the car. However, the car did not move forward.

"Mummy, today I brought a surprise for you...... The tasty cream cake that mummy brought this morning for me."

John took one of the reserved cakes and put it in the mummy's mouth. Mummy ate it with a small smile, then another one for John too.

"John, wear your seatbelt "

"Okay mummy "John continued.

" I have something important to say to my mummy. Will you hear it?"

"Okay, let me hear... you say that"

" I love you, mummy,......"

"Me too, baby,......."

John also did not forget to look at the school for the last time as it began to fade away from him.

"Bye... bye... I like to see you soon, as soon as possible...." suddenly John turned to mummy,

"Mummy, where are we going now?"

"For shopping."

" Oh yes,... Can you buy me one shoe? please mummy,... I love you,......"

Mummy looked at John with a smile and John looked at mummy with a great embarrassment.

The car sped forward quickly reversing its surroundings......

CHAPTER TWO

The sky is trying to escape into the Darkness on a cloudy evening, and there are indications of light rain all around. Shows a very cute little boy holding his mummy's hand and walking, he is very happy because today is his last school day and tomorrow morning he and his mummy have to go to see his distant daddy.

Both are very much in love with their only son, 'John', and the same goes for John too.

John loves his daddy very much even though he sees his dad occasionally. John is Forbidden in everything while living with his mummy, but daddy is not like that, because John can do whatever he wants and will do whatever he says.

Yet John's mind was full of only his mummy, more than his daddy.

"My sweet mummy"

John's gait, which was very happy, has changed. Instead of walking obediently, he jumps and runs to move forward but Mummy often forbids it.

" Keep your gait... otherwise you will get beat by me."

But John deliberately blew his mummy's warning into the air because he knows that mummy likes his walk and that mummy struggles to stop her laughing at his walk even when she is angry.

Mummy can tell from his character that he is full of joy because he has a nice journey tomorrow and is also in a hurry to see daddy.

What memories John is going to get from daddy, buying chocolates, taking him on trips, teaching him gun shooting, taking him shopping and taking him to the swimming pool, and so on.

Mummy knows very well that all the thoughts about these are shining in his eyes, so mummy did not want to be a hindrance to his happiness.

The two of them approach the car and mummy opens the dickey and puts the shopping items safely in place, this time John runs and settles down next to mummy, just before mummy.

John looked up and saw a sight as he glanced around.

A begging grandmother and a very pretty little girl next to that grandmother. John remembered the name with a shock, **"Donna,...."**

His eyes filled with tears, Suddenly he heard the door open, and his attention shifted to the mummy.

" What happened sweetie, ...? why are you crying? Mummy inquired.

"Nothing mummy..... I love you, so"

But mummy also did not forget to give a kiss.

Mummy started to pick up the car, but suddenly mummy stopped the car when she heard someone calling behind.

That was the car keeper, "Madam, this is your car parking charge."

John got this opportunity, and soon he rolled his eyes at Donna again.

"Donna, I will be back, and I will express my love for you to my mummy and daddy, and they will marry you to me, but I am pretty sorry because I'm going to miss you now...."

The car sped forward.

The cloud is darkened, the sun is about to set, birds are hurrying to get somewhere, and farmers are returning to work in the field after a small rain. Therefore It may have been the atmosphere after a little rain.

John looked out, soon the he cool breeze kissed him and passed by, yes.... It has rained, and the wetness and cold in the surroundings are proof of that.

It is not known whether it is closer to night or the clouds cover the sun. However, the sky is still dark.

Trying to calm everything down is like going back to sleep, But, ...The car moved forward crossing everyone and everything.

Arriving home, mummy is busy with packing all the things she needs to take tomorrow and the gift to surprise daddy. But something was bothering him in John's mind and John had a bad time thinking about going tomorrow.

Even if he doesn't want to go, it is not possible at all. The excitement in his mind about the journey of tomorrow is fading now. John walked over to the nearest window, raised his eyes to the sky and took a deep breath, and then became silent.

The sun is dying in the sky, and the birds follow the path to death to die with the dying sun.

John was watching all this very carefully.

"John, it is time for dinner", mummy's voice scared John a little.

" Okay, Mummy I am coming...."

John looked at the stars that appeared in the sky for the last time and then went out for food.

He secured his place at the dining table.

"What food will Donna eat...? Can Donna eat such good food like mine?"

John often cries before eating, but mummy was pleasantly surprised to see his changes in behavior today.

After dinner, he went to bed in his room, but couldn't sleep. John felt as if the moon in the sky was only looking at him through the window. That sight made him feel a little uncomfortable.

Thoughts, desire, and fear passed through his mind that night.

"Why John, have you not slept yet?

Try to go to bed, we have to leave early tomorrow morning."

"Mummy, I can't sleep"

"Why sweetie,...?"

"Let me ask mummy one thing?",

"Yes, sure baby you can."

" That is.... Mummy.... Can...."

John needed to talk about something urgent, but his tongue was not moving a little, and John was totally confused and did not know what to talk about.

"I am not coming tomorrow Mummy, because I do not want to go tomorrow."

"Why are you talking like this now, John? "

"Mummy, what is wrong with Donna?"

"Oh she,..... she,..... is.." mummy started to say something.

"Donna's mummy is very upset because she cannot see her husband for the last time, but now she is acting like she is seeing her husband everywhere.

So, Donna is cared for by their grandmother, not by Donna's mummy. Anyway, the doctor said that her mother could not come back to her old ways. So, grandma and

Donna beg on the roadside to pay for the house's needs."

Mummy continued, "The old grandmother has a lot of physical problems and illnesses,...Poor Donna,' God would have shown this fate to that cute baby at such a young age,....."

After saying this, the mummy remained silent.

"Mummy, I love Donna very much,..." Mummy smiled when she heard his harsh words and told,

"Only good people can love those who have no one. You, too, are a good person."

"No Mummy. I mean,..... (silent)

"Okay John, you don't have to worry, close your eyes and try to sleep fast."

After turning off the lamplight and kissing John, the Mummy walked back from there.

Tears flowed from his eyes as if it were a spring on cliffs.

Again he concentrated his view on the outside moon as before.

"Sorry donna, I cannot miss you, if no one is with you don't worry because I am always with you."

John's eyes lit for a moment and then later slowly closed, John slipped into the Valley of Sleep with the dream he will never forget, without assurance of expectations.

John wakes up after hearing his mummy's words," It is time to get up and go quickly."

But John turned to sleep, not listening to mummy's words.

" Please open the door to the bathroom at last."

Hearing Mummy's loud voice, John came out of his sleep and was shocked. John looked around because he was totally confused.

"When did I lie in the bathtub?"

Suddenly some past things ran through his mind, John was terrified when he remembered what had happened just before.

He approached the door in the bathroom with shaky legs. The hands are shaking and doesn't have the courage to open, and the experience once it's opened is beyond what he can expect even though soon he unlocked the door without thinking.

John opened the door and saw his tired mummy.

"Mummy I really,... sorry,... I didn't know."

With a smile, mummy took him and entered the bathroom.

"Mummy, do not give me a bath in cold water in the morning," John begged.

But mummy did not pretend to hear those words.

John lost his sleep because of the mummy, so John decided not to talk to the mummy but with mummy kissed him, and John's decision vanished.

Time had passed but sleep had not changed from his eyes.

Mummy kept John safe inside the car and soon after, mummy drove the car forward.

"Mummy, what is the time now?" John asked drowsily.

"Morning 2 o'clock" mummy answered.

With a jolt, John asked mummy, "Did you wake me up so early?"

" No baby, the flight is at 3 o'clock and today I seem to be late anyway."

The car sped off knocking out the cold darkness with the wipers. mummy wiped the snow from the car windows from time to time.

John's seat was a little higher so that John could see the outside views.

The light on in every house that he knew outside was off, which meant they were in deep sleep and the farmers he saw yesterday are not taking any work now, and they too are now in deep sleep.

John deliberately wanted to sleep like one of them but still, John was very interested in the outside views.

Houses and trees were hidden in the dark, no one around, John realized that there would be only silence around.

His visibility was limited for a short time due to the speed of the car but the sights remained in his mind for a long time. John was more eager to wipe out the cold that stuck to the window and see that the field he saw yesterday was now silent with no one.

It seemed to John that he could only hear the fast sound of his car in a quiet atmosphere.

He's always seen in these ways, yet he doesn't know why, and now he's more close to this place he's so familiar with than on other days.

So he's a little worried about his journey ahead of his way out of here, and John looks at mummy as if to say this, but mummy is too busy, he has lost both the mind to tell and the mind to say goodbye to Mummy.

"Mummy, I'm not coming... I don't want to leave here and go to see daddy."

Hearing this, mummy pressed the brakes of the car quickly. John leaned forward as if to fall because the brakes were pressed so quickly, he was able to avoid an unexpected accident because as early as mummy put the seat belt on John and tightened him.

"Okay my sweetie, I'll set the way home on the GPS.I'll probably be late to see daddy today...I want to see your dad anyway. So you follow this GPS and go home. I've kept all the food you need in the fridge."

John's happiness could not be limited because of the mummy's positive words he never expected.

John immediately said goodbye to Mummy and got out of the car, and Mummy said goodbye to him and jumped forward.

John stared blankly until Mummy's car disappeared from his sight, though he could not see mummy.

Now Mummy was not near him but this walk alone did not frighten him.

All that was left for John around was the dim light so that John could see exactly the way forward.

As mummy said John is progressing based on GPS but his eyes are unknowingly immersed in the beauty of nature because he does not need this GPS, this beautiful nature will tell him the right way home.

Protected the cold as hysterical as the breeze trying to pass accidentally collided with John,... But John was affectionate in that little mistake.

Some of the faint voices trying to follow in John's footsteps, John was not ready to look back because his goal was home.

But this is where John must have done a little stupid thing, and some unexpected sound came to John's ears and it was just behind John as if it were a sign.

John mustered up the courage and tried to look back as if to see it, but before his eyes could fully capture the scene, the headlight of the vehicle behind him slammed into John's eyes and passed quickly.

" **Mummy,....** "

"John,..John,.. What happened? What's wrong with you,...? "

The same mummy's voice that he thought had gone away echoed in his ears again.

John is still in the car, but John understands nothing.

His eyes sharped to the back as he recognized something, and a big truck that had begun to disappear from his eyes as if it were the last, but John could not take his eyes off that distant truck.

Seeing his skeptical look, Mummy seemed to understand something and Mummy started talking to him,

"Oh, John, Is that what scares you? That truck passed us so fast. Actually, I was also scared at first when I saw its arrival....Anyway, my sweetie need not be afraid because your mummy is driving, so you are safe...."

Mummy's affectionate eyes were fixed on him, and though he did not reply to mummy's words, his eyes filled with tears without him realizing it.

John wants to see many things but before that, he is dragged into the darkness. John opened his eyes when he heard mummy calling his name.

John realized he had arrived at the airport and by then the toll gate had been crossed.

Mummy Parked the car in a place.

"Sir, I think we will be late for the flight today, please don't tell me to put the car away, " mummy requested.

The car keeper said with a smile, "No matter, you don't worry about it. I will keep this car till you come, I can understand your situation."

"Thank you so much, sir..." Mummy quickly took her luggage and walked to the airport, followed by John.

"Walk fast John "Mummy argued.

"Don't talk to me angrily, I don't like it" John warns Mummy.

"Oops sorry sweetie,... I apologize for my mistake,...Can you please walk fast,...?"

He liked what mummy said jokingly.

John could see the car Parker disappearing into the darkness.

" Okay uncle, I will bring candy for you when I come back."

Mummy run to reception, "Hello madam, good morning,... Airbus number...... When will this flight depart?"

"Is your flight at 3 o'clock?" the reception lady asked.

"Yes that is",.....mummy nodded.

"Sorry madam, the flight is getting ready to take off, if you had come a little earlier I would have gotten you there somehow."

Mummy got very tired of their words and her eyes fell on John. He noticed that his mummy's eyes were filling up but soon his eyes slightly filled too.

But unexpectedly a smile spread across the mummy's face, but it was just made.

After a short silence mummy again continued,

"It is okay, Leena,....Will there be any other flights now...? It has been a long time since I saw my husband. So... anyway I urgently need to go see my husband today."

"Okay Lilly, I can understand your feelings, I will try my best."

The reception girl continued.

"Oh yes you are lucky, if you wait half an hour, I can book a seat for you on a late flight but this flight does not go directly to your destination and you don't have to pay any more money. I will manage it."

"Okay Leena, we will be on that same flight no matter what."

mummy said, glancing at John.

"Ok Lilly, I can book a seat for you soon. then,... I miss you a lot."

"Me to Leena. I will never forget your favor,...." Mummy added.

After talking, mummy walked out of the reception to a nearby seat, then the luggage was safely put away. John followed the mummy.

" Who is mummy Leena,... mummy's friend?" John asked.

"Yes John, when I was a child, she was my best friend and she was with me until I was in 4th grade, after 4th grade I joined a school abroad with my mum and I have been separating her ever since, and now I see Leena again, when I was with her, I shared all my worries in my mind only with her and she is a better sister than a friend of mine. Isn't that why she understood me so quickly now,......?"

"Was Mummy a kid like me in the past?"

"Yes John, I was...."

He could not believe it and asked mummy the same question over and over again.

"Yes John, I was a kid first too then I grew up and now I have a baby and you will have a baby when you grow up tomorrow."

But he now cried when he heard his mummy's words because he always wanted to be his mummy's baby.

"All right, John. No,.. Never,... You will not grow up, you will always be my baby". Now John was relieved to hear Mummy's words.

After taking a deep breath, mummy continued again.

"Do you have such good friends, John?"

"Yes mummy, she is Donna. John said with a slight blush. Smiling mummy asked, "Then?"

After saying this, John's eyes got a little wet.

"John, why are you crying?"

"Nothing Mummy,... I had a wish to see the place where Donna was sitting but I forgot in my sleep..... When can I see her again....? When will I be back,...?" John asked anxiously.

Unexpectedly, a bag fell loudly from the hand of someone who had passed just behind John, **but the bag wasn't broken.**

Frightened by this unexpected sudden sound, John hugged Mummy tightly, but since the bag fell just behind John, he was not particularly injured.

Mummy must have been frightened when she heard this sound because Mummy too hugged John tightly.

"Oops...little sweetie, Are you scared,..?"

John nodded his head with filling eyes.

"Don't worry,... Nothing,... You are safe now. "

Mummy was so kind to him at those times that she felt so kind to him that she put him close to her chest and now he realized that he was closest to mummy's heart.

Mummy fell asleep while waiting for the next flight.

While sleeping, Leena came tired to knock mummy up.

Lilly,... Lilly... wake up... I have something very important to tell you."

Mummy woke up a little shocked from her sleep and asked,

"What is the matter,.."

" That is,... Lilly..." Leena could not say anything.

"No matter, tell me what the matter is," Mummy asked again.

"The situation of the flight you're going to travel on is not very pleasant because the emergency landing was made twice before it reached the airport.. That is why,...

"Was that it,...? Don't worry"

Mummy's voice stumbled a little.

Leena continued, Lilly, if you've been waiting a while I can book a direct flight and I will take all the expenses, please come tomorrow at the exact time. Mummy turned and looked at John.

"Oh...this is not something that happens and he is a changing character, no matter Leena I decided to go on my current flight.....Have you booked that flight,...?" Mummy asked.

" Yes... I have given your name." Lenna replayed.

Mummy continued,

"I cannot wait to see my husband until tomorrow because I told my husband that we would arrive tonight. The main purpose of my departure was to tell my husband something important."

John was very attentive to his mummy's words and all of the mummy's words were kept in his little heart.

"yes Lilly, I can understand but it is better to think and do."

" Never mind,... I doubt I will come back here with my son tomorrow, "mummy looked at John with a smiling face.

"Oh my GOD, was this your son.....? I am paying attention to him now. Why didn't you tell me about your son?"

Lilly hugged her son and gave him a smirk on his cheek and said,

"Yes, he is my first son"

"Yes Lilly, it is so cute to see your son"

John noticed the smile on auntie's face too, he hugged his mummy with a little embarrassment.

"Leena, where are your children?" Mummy asked.

"I don't have children. Doctors say there is no chance of having children"

"Oops, sorry dear I didn't know"

"It's okay, what about your family?

suddenly a call made a hindrance to their conversation.

"Hay Lenna...",

They both turned their attention when they heard someone calling.

Suddenly Leena got up and started to leave.

"Okay Lilly,...continue,... All the best"

Soon, Leena disappeared through the crowd and the mummy kept watching until Leena and Aunty disappeared.

"What was the secret mummy?" John asked anxiously.

"Oh that is,... That is a surprise for you and your dad.....Think about what that would be?

" Sure, I will find out what it is," John promised mummy.

John noticed the crowds moving around him, and they were happy, even though they were very busy.

John can understand the secret of happiness on the faces of most of them because he is experiencing the same happiness now.

Time was moving forward a lot, and John was tired of looking around for a long time, so he turned to mummy.

"How long do we have to wait for the flight, Mummy,...? Because I am so tired,....."

Mummy got up and brought a storybook and a round cake from a nearby shop and gave it to John.

"A KID UNDER THE TWO WOLVES"

He read the letters written on the outside of the book effortlessly and John was very surprised by the picture outside the book.

"Mummy, will wolves have a love for humans or children?"

Mummy laughed at his serious question but she did not want to scare her son.

"Yes baby,...Yes,. You are right, Wolves love people, especially children.

Suddenly, the announcement of the scheduled flight was heard all over the place. Mummy and John quickly stepped forward. John kept the book very carefully in the small bag that mummy had brought for him.

From time to time John made sure it was inside the bag because what the mummy brought was always so precious to John.

"It is my ticket and,... I have my son with me" Mummy told the lady.

"Yes, thank you. Madam, you wait here till we finish checking" John is looking at all this with surprise and his mind was filled with the excitement of seeing his daddy today, his mummy knows this too.

John looked at each of the people there and said, "When will I see you all again?"

"Sorry madam, we will not let you go," The security lady said.

Suddenly a shock passed mummy and John.

"Why,...why are you saying that?" Mummy asked angrily.

"Because, we have not received any information about your child,.... Where is his ticket?"

"His ticket is,... "Mummy searched the whole bag but his ticket was nowhere to be found.

Mummy stopped searching and froze as if she realized something.

"Sorry madam, I did not book the seat, it was my friend in the reception so she only knew about me but she didn't know about my son before,... and I think she forgot about my son while talking to me"

Mummy said, she didn't want to stop.

Mummy continued, "Madam, I missed my first flight. I can only go on this one flight, I need to see my husband somehow tomorrow and please allow us to log in anyway." Mummy pleaded with them.

John was also so upset by the mummy's condition that his eyes were filled with ignorance.

"Don't worry madam, you can go but keep this card in your hand before you leave because if there's any problem, you just have to show it"

John and mummy were relieved to hear this positive answer.

After a while of waiting, they were both allowed to enter and they had no limit to their joy when they heard this good news.

"Thank you so much, I will never forget this favor"

"Welcome, happy journey "

"What time will we get there tomorrow?" Mummy inquired.

" First you'll land at an airport and then you will take a flight to your destination and you have the facility to take the rest there....The flight will depart from there only after a while. So if you ask in detail when you will arrive, we cannot give any proper answer"

"John's business, I am not going to take the risk", mummy said to John gently patting him on the white cheek.

"What mummy, what is the matter"?

"No, nothing sweetie, we might have to wait for some time inside the flight itself"

"It is okay mummy, it is not a problem" John mumbled too.

Mummy walked forward holding his hand and looked back as if suddenly remembering something while walking.

"**Leena,....**" he could hear mummy's lips whispering and he realized that mummy was only looking back to see Leena.

"You were my best friend and beyond all my good sister and you were the only one who loved me in my childhood. I had no one but you. It was only through you until I learned what love is but I had to part with you. I apologize to you for everything but in the end, I thought you would come to see me but now I realize that you don't love me as much as I love you."

Mummy suddenly turned to John and realized that he had heard everything she said. Mummy hugged the crying John.

"Sorry sweetie,... I forgot for a moment that you are there."

"Mummy,... I love you very much, even though no one loves you. John told with weeping eyes.

"Yes, I know that, my sweetie. Come on let us go"

"Mummy, why are you still crying?"

John asked as he walked.

"Nothing baby, I cried unknowingly in the joy of seeing daddy tomorrow" Mummy answered.

"Does anyone cry when happiness comes? " John asked a big question.

"Yes sure, even when we are happy we will cry without realizing it." mummy replied.

"How?" John could not believe it.

"We cry when we have unbearable sorrow. If so, why not cry when we have unbearable joy?"

John looked at Mummy with suspicion but Mummy continued again with a smile,"We cry unknowingly when there are difficulties that we can't bear. It's the same when we have unbearable happiness that we cry without knowing it."

John knows very well that mummy won't look back anyway, so John slowly turned his back.

At the same time John had seen aunty watching them from the crowd.

"What was auntie's name...? Oops I forgot,....Yes, mummy's best friend,... John struggled to remember.

Aunty seems to be crying, and seeing this john tried to call mummy but aunty showed John the sign language that, "Don't call her"

"Mummy, look at that,... **'Leena aunty'**.."

John said unknowingly but he did not know how he came to remember that forgotten name now.

Mummy quickly turned around when she heard 'Leena' but mummy did not see Leena in the crowd.

"What John,...Are you kidding...?"

Mummy unknowingly raised her voice but suddenly looked at John and smiled.

"You are starting to lie a bit recently" mummy said lovingly, patting John on the head.

"Mummy, I was right what I said, Leena aunty was there," John said repeatedly.

"Sometimes it will be your feeling," Mummy said.

John again looked back and noticed that Leena aunty was still there at the same place but this time he did not tell mummy that because mummy was arguing with him because of Leena aunty.

After completing the final checking, John and Mummy stepped closer to the flight.

John was surprised to see large planes lined up around him.

Despite having so many flights around, John already knew which flight they were going to take. John was paying special attention to the large Crowd trying to board the same flight they were to take.

He was alight with the hope of getting to see daddy as he got close to the flight.

While he walks, John tries to read the large English letters written on the outside of the flight.

A cool breeze swept past John, he took a deep breath of cool breeze, As if giving him new energy, he opened his eyes. All his remaining happy moments passed through his mind.

Happiness was on the faces of everyone trying to board the flight, all of them are probably going to their loved ones. like us,... John understood.

Mummy got her seat on the side of a window, and he ran away and sat in that seat. Mummy kissed John and put the seat belt on him.

The flight was about to take off, and the air hostesses were giving classes on how to wear an oxygen mask and how to use the parachute but he rejected the classes as much as attending classes at regular School. John was particularly careful to see an air hostess in it like his maths teacher.

John looked around, everyone was listening intently to the classes.

He decided to act like them because everyone was listening to those classes.

Unexpectedly a message came on the mummy's phone, it was an unknown number and John was the first to see the message, he tried to read the text and gave it to the mummy.

Mummy was reading those messages, and at that moment she was motivated to fill her eyes.

"Hello,... hi, I am Leena,...

Your son was right, I was standing there looking at you and when you turned back I hid from there because I love you so much and I thought I should not be a hindrance to the joy of seeing your husband.

When I am with you, you will travel to the memories and I know very well about your memories,...... Anyway, I have one thing to tell you that is we should never fall into the memories, only need to be remembered, just as a past.

But anyway, I know you want to have a relationship with me again, you are my best friend. never be, you are my best sister more than a best friend.

Don't feel bad for me for not seeing you for the last time,.... don't feel bad for this poor Leena, bye... bye...I love you soo,......"

The suppressed mummy's tears crossed the boundaries and came out, mummy tried to stop it with her hand but it was in vain. When Mummy's eyes filled up, John's eyes filled up too. Even though mummy looked at him and smiled, he couldn't smile back at mummy.

The engine's noise began to double, and the air hostess asked everyone to ensure their seat belt.

The flight began to move slowly, John felt as if his Joy exploded inside him and he looked at those around him and realized that they were the same but mummy wasn't like that.

John could have particularly understood the speed of running down the flight runway.

When he last saw each of the vehicles and people who were speeding behind him, he would ask himself,

" When will I see you again?"

Suddenly the flight took off into the sky in a shock, this is the moment that John found most terrifying.

"Mummy,...When will we be back here?"

"Everything will be alright to you when you see your Daddy", mummy said.

John took the book out of his little bag and began to read. Mummy was also a little surprised to see John's routine changes.

"A KID UNDER THE TWO WOLVES "

John whispered.

He was flipping through every page of the book to see something more favorable to him.

"This book is full of writing and there is not even a single picture,...?"

John told his complaint to mummy.

But looking at mummy, the mummy was asleep. He knew full well that waking up mummy would cause an argument, so he did not try.

"Yes idea,...let's see how many pages are in this book," John told himself.

"One,... Two,... Three,...four,... Ten,... "He began to count each page.

Everyone's attention in the plane was diverted to John without them even knowing it.

"A very cute little boy"

But John doesn't notice any of the changes in his surroundings because of him, because he is immersed in his serious work.

Suddenly there was a big shake on the flight and his book fell down with a loud thud. Mummy woke up in shock and she picked up the book lying on the floor and looked at John angrily but he couldn't bear to see mummy's angrily look.

"I did nothing, the book fell out of my hand unknowingly when the flight got stuck", his eyes began to wet and the tears streamed down his cheeks and his face turned to red.

Wiping away tears and he said,

"I don't like you because you don't know how to behave towards the baby children,..."

Mummy smiled when she heard his words and she looked at John and closed her eyes.

"Sorry dear, you don't care it, you are my baby ever "

It is a great relief for him when he sees the behavior of the loving mummy after her anger. He nodded at the mummy's request.

John wiped away the tears and said,

"Mummy, did you think the flight was broken,......? "

This question shook mummy a lot.

But to keep John from being intimidated, mummy muttered, "Hey,....No....Nothing like that."

Mummy closed her eyes pretending to be asleep not wanting to talk anymore but John was not ready to keep quiet, some questions that were hidden inside John came out for the answer.

"Mummy, I heard Leena aunty say this flight will crash,... Then will we all die? "

Suddenly, Mummy woke up, covered his mouth and gestured to lower his voice.

"My sweetie will never die. I will save you wherever you are and always will be with you even if I die" mummy replied.

"It is never going to be like what mummy says. Sure I will die if my mummy dies because I cannot live without my sweet mummy". John said with trembling lips and filling eyes.

Mummy patted him on the cheek and said, "God doesn't do anything like that in our lives, therefore don't be afraid,... I will be with you till the end."

John again wiped away his tears and told mummy with a smile that, "I love you mummy,.... so much...."

Mummy gestured for an air hostess in front of them to come over.

"Hello, madam, how much longer is the first landing? Mummy asked.

" Madam, it is likely to arrive at the next airport in an hour "

"Why,... Are there any problems with the flight...? Is that why you land there?" Mummy asked.

"That,... That is,... We don't know and it is landing for checking, if there are no problems the flight will take off in minutes." Said the air hostess.

"That means, you're saying there is something wrong with this flight?"

"No madam, you don't have to worry. It is all over and It is the duty of the pilots to bring you safely to your destination. They are not the ones who worked as pilots yesterday or today, they have a year of experience. However, if the flight doesn't fly now then the company will face a loss of dollars," the air hostess added.

The words of the air hostess seemed to encourage mummy because mummy didn't ask any more questions.

John was listening to this without his mummy knowing, he looked around and there were little kids, old people, young people, and young women, so many,... All of them had happy reasons hidden on their faces.

" Mummy, would we die if we fell from such a height? " He asked mummy.

"Never sweetie,... We can get away and nothing like that can happen in our lives"

After a short break, Mommy hurried to talk to him again, "John,..... Did you see that baby..? and you want to have a baby like that...? "

"I want to,..." John nodded.

John again continued,

"And mummy,... I have a doubt.. If I had a sister or brother, wouldn't daddy and mummy love me less?" He said with a breaking voice.

Mummy laughed when she heard this.

"No matter how many God gives me, I will love all babies in the same way"

"How do mummy, babies come to be,...And who will give us children?" John raised his question.

"God,... God decided who should live on the earth and who should not". And children can only be born if two loving people marry each other" Mummy added.

"Oh I see,..." John thought about Donna for a moment.

" Where will Donna be now....? I'm on the flight now and Donna is begging there sometime. Poor donna,... If only she was my sister,... Oh,... No... no,...if she was my wife, I would have hugged her and kissed her a lot. "

"What do you think?" Mummy asked.

"Nothing mummy,.." John said with shock.

"Can I marry someone?"

"No,... Never,..." mummy closed her eyes.

"No,... I meant a small child, not a big one,..." He continued.

"No,... No one can marry anyone without coming age" while saying this mummy was struggling to stop her laughing, John understood.

"So when will I get married? " John asked.

"We will arrange a wedding for you when you are twenty-five years old," Mummy said with a smile.

"**Twenty-five**,... Oh my God,... Do I have to be that old?" He asked mummy without being believed.

"Yes that much,"... Mummy said firmly.

"What would happen if I got married before that age? "

"The cops will catch it,... Those are one of the big crimes and also their parents will be in prison for a long time,...."

John never expected this answer to come out of his mummy's mouth and soon he was overwhelmed with grief and anger and resentment.

"Mummy,... I like Donna.... Can I marry her...?"

John asked mummy very loudly, shaking the whole flight.

Quickly mummy covered his mouth and urged him to keep quiet, and the eyes of those around her turned to mummy but with a simple smile, mummy ignored them all.

But shame was still reflected on the mummy's face. However, John continued, "What I said It's true".

"John,...Listen to me. Donna is a fatherless child that is why You need to see her as your own sister. We need to feel sorry for her. I noticed you were crying when I started to get up from your room after talking about Donna yesterday, and I also noticed you looking at Donna many times when you went to school with me, but I thought you may see that little girl as your own sister."

After a silence mummy again continued, "Can such desires occur at such a young age?" mummy asked herself looking at little John.

"Mummy,...... I cannot miss Donna because I loved her so much"

Mummy continues with a smile, "It doesn't matter if you love her now because you and she are still small children and now you cannot marry her,....Then,... If you still like her, keep it up and study well, we will marry her to you when she and you grow up.... and then I love Donna too, I saw her as my one baby and I would tell daddy about her and we thought about adopting her".

Mummy, who had begun to say something, suddenly looked at John and was stunned.

"Oh no,... No matter what, you're a child and you do not know what you are saying or doing right now"

"No mummy,.. everything I know,.. Then mummy, what does adoption mean?"

"Oh,... is that, if I say it now you will not understand therefore I will tell you when you grow up."

The announcement rang out on the flight to make the flight land, soon the flight flew down to the earth very quickly and crossed the runway, and then slowly stopped.

"Mummy,.. will it be too late for us to see daddy again....? Will we have to stay here too long....?"

"Maybe so sweetie, anyways it is good for all of us to stay here and we will be safe even if we have to wait a while." Mummy replied.

John runs his eyes around, some of them reading books, some of them talking to others and some are sleeping, but no one questioned, "Why did the flight land here? "Because everyone was engrossed in their affairs.

"Anyway Mummy,... We missed the first flight because of me and if it was the first flight, we could have reached daddy earlier now...But..."

Unable to finish what was said, his voice cut in half.

" You don't have to worry about it anymore my sweaty,.. from now onward you should always be serious and be aware of what we need to do next and you have to fight or survive in any situation in life. Do you understand what I am saying?" After a short silence mummy resumed.

"No matter, you are a little boy therefore I know you do not understand what I just said, however, you must keep this in your mind when an adversity strikes in your life and you must remember my words and move on" mummy advised John as if he needed something.

John didn't understand what mummy said but what she said caught his mind and John shook his head in silence.

"Hello dear passengers, we're going to take off the flight in a while and we have just landed here for emergency landing and we found out there's no problem with this flight in the mechanical test. Therefore,... the flight will take off immediately without much delay"

There was a great murmur among the passengers, "What did the flight land in?"

Some people looked at their watch and started to become tense.

At that time a Businessman got up and said very loudly, "Today I had a very urgent meeting but most likely I will be late to get there"

"Sorry sir, your safety is the first thing we're giving priority to", the air hostess said.

When heard this, mummy looked at the air hostess slightly because Leena had already told her about this flight.

"Maybe it is an emergency landing, that is why they told us to wait a while without agreeing to let any people go out."

"They may not have tested the flight sometime"

"Can they test the flight so quickly?"

"Yes,... Yes,... You're right, I am also very suspicious of their words" the conversations among the passengers fell on mummy's ears.

"Yes,.. you are right, they are trying to hide something from us and they are doing this for their profit," Another man told them from behind.

Mummy and John listened to their conversations.

"Mummy,... I am so scared, are we going to die?" John asked, trembling with fear.

"Never baby,... Don't be scared,... If pilots were sure this flight would be in danger, would they come with us on the same flight? mummy asked John.

"Never,... Mummy's right,...John answered.

"The flight is about to take off,... Everyone, please wear seat belts." one of the air hostess said.

Everyone stopped their discussions and turned ready to wear their seat belts.

Mummy made sure that she wore John's seat belt properly and soon John took a look at Mummy.

"Mummy,... by leaving here so early, we can see daddy earlier. right?." John told mummy with a smile on his face but mummy's face was not so happy.

"What mummy,....? What's up,...?Aren't you happy to see daddy,...?"

"Nothing baby,... I am glad to see daddy too." mummy said in a small voice.

John could see the guilt on mummy's face that she had made the wrong decision to come on this flight. Mummy looked out of the window and it looked like all of her hopes had been dashed because by which time the flight had taken its extreme speed before the flight and soon within seconds the flight rose from the ground into the sky with more force and with a shudder.

John looked out of the window and was amazed to see every object, peoples, vehicle, tree, and building that quickly disappeared from his view.

John noticed that as it rose from the earth, everything became small lines and specks.

"How big they were,... and how small they are now, "John murmured.

Slowly the clouds covered the flight completely and the flight began to move forward through the clouds slowly.

During this time the cloud hit the window and shattered into tiny pieces and spread away.

Everything was very close to his sight and he was watching all these wonderful and everlasting experiences without even realizing that the time is passing him fastly.

Without too long he realized an unexplainable silence filled the entire flight because everyone was asleep and as he remembered something he turned to the mummy and realized that mummy was also a member of that silence.

John suddenly looked back as if he remembered something, the angry Businessman was also asleep now like everyone and by seeing this he felt a little relieved because earlier John was afraid of his loud voice.

Now only the sound of the flight was heard all around and the sound of nothing else annoying there but these moments scares him a little.

John realized that everyone except himself had fainted into the silence, the elderly grandmother and grandfather in the front seat, the small two children and their mummy in the middle seat, and those young guys just right to him, all fainted in the silence, even his mummy too.

John could not get anyone else up but he tried to get his mummy up because he was so afraid of this situation but he could not get up even with his mummy because he felt as if something was blocking his little hands.

And he also wanted to be a member of the silent and he tried to doze off in silence the same as others but could not.

He looked up again to the two little ones nearby, they were also asleep.

"Why am I not the only one sleeping?" John asked himself.

Suddenly a question that arose inside his mind passed at the lightning speed,

"Could the Pilots have fallen asleep in the fearful silence?"

Unfortunately, the emergency alarm on the flight suddenly turned on and the red light inside the flight hurt his eyes. Everyone who fell asleep got up in fear and asked the air hostess about "what is going on here right now,"

The air hostess, who was drowsy, got up quickly and ran to the cockpit.

But the returning hostess had no words to say while trying to say their words were stumbling.

Mummy understood everything when she saw their guilty face and mummy said aloud,

"This was an emergency landing twice before I boarded this flight and they hid the fact from us that there was a mechanical problem with the flight... and I am sure that they skipped the mechanical test to adjust the timing of the flight."

"Who told you about this?" One of the passengers asked his mummy nervously.

"A friend of mine told me about this.She works as a receptionist at the airport where I boarded" But Mummy could not finish her words because before that one of the air hostesses started talking very angrily to everyone,

"If she already knew this flight was dangerous, Why would she have boarded this flight?" The air hostess asked everyone very loudly.

Then again the air hostess continued,

"Please never believe any of the lies she tells because I'm sure she's a bitch." They yelled angrily, and some of the air hostesses looked at Mummy and mocked her.

Mummy angrily slammed into the front seat when she heard what they were saying. The whole front seat shook by the force of her blows.

"Yes, she was right. I was a lunatic so I decided to come on this flight. Many times my friend forced me not to take this flight but I decided to come on the same flight only because I was crazy and I wanted so much to see my husband who had been separated for a long time..... but I still glorify God that I may not be able to see my husband again but it doesn't a matter because I am still the only one left to tell you this truth."

John, his eyes were stitched up towards his mummy and he was so stunned that he could not believe his eyes because this was the first time he had seen mummy so angry.

"What they did to us was an extreme deception". Voices were raised from many quarters.

The businessman, terrified to hear what was happening here, rushed forward to beat someone on the air hostess but some passengers blocked the businessman who was coming forward.

"Please do not do anything like that right now,...Let's see first if something happens or not." One of the passengers said loudly to everyone and most agreed with what was said and some were still skeptical but fear of death was still on the faces of those who agreed.

The flight showed many dangerous signs even though the flight was still normal at that time.

The Air hostess asked for everyone to remain silent so that the flight began to achieve total silence again.

But,...

There was a big shake-up in the flight, shattering everyone's silence.

As the flight shook violently, something very heavy fell from above on to one man without leaving even a last breath. Soon he was crushed under it and his blood spilled on John's face.

All that was left was a very unexpected thing and everyone who saw such a terrifying sight immediately panicked and became crazy just not knowing where to go or what to do.

Due to the occasional shaking, the luggage stored on the top fell very hard on the people's heads.

On seeing this, mummy quickly stood up and threw all her luggage to somewhere that was just above John's head and from there mummy took a new big bag as if it were necessary.

"What is mummy doing?" he wanted to ask but neither his tongue nor his hand was moving.

One of the air hostesses pulled and opened the cockpit door but meanwhile, a pilot fell out as half burnt from inside but he was still alive.

"There is no reason to expect it anymore,.... everyone's going to die,... The Pilot to control this flight is also near to die,...."

Someone yelled from somewhere in shock and passengers tried to push themselves through the running fire.

No one had time to do anything in advance during these unexpected situations.

Many people started jumping out the door of the flight because of the assurance of being in the throes of death and during that rush, some of them fell down without being able to move on.

There was a grandmother among them but no one noticed her who had fallen and John realized that she might have wanted help but the grandfather couldn't do anything special when he came close to grandmother.

After looking at the fallen grandmother for a moment, the grandfather took the grandmother as if something had been fixed in his mind and walked calmly into the blazing fire but still the grandfather could not walk at all, John realized, soon that the fire must have understood these difficulty being faced by grandfather so soon it swallowed both of them quickly.

Tears fell from John's eyes when he saw this mind-blowing sight and he could not tell mummy to save them because his tongue and whole body were motionless.

Suddenly he heard mummy's voice from behind and turned around. Mummy was trying very hard to tell John something but John tried to understand even though her words stumbled.

"John, please hear what I am saying,... listen to me,you must have got into this bag and I have tied a rope through this bag from outside and its remaining I set it inside....Now I'm gonna throw you down because I am sure that you will come down safely because of the trees below and then you should pull the rope from inside.... then the bag will come to open. Okay,... did you understand?"

"Hmm,... Mummy?"

But mummy continued saying these same words over and over again.

Then mummy, what is next,....? John asked mummy very angrily but mummy couldn't say anything in the face of his question.

Soon he hugged her slightly silent and he realized that his pressure while hugging made mummy hard and it might have choked mummy a little.

"If mummy is not with me, I won't go anywhere. Come with me Mummy, No you must have to come." John insisted.

"John, please you understand what I am saying and you are my sweet baby forever anyway, sure I will return as soon as possible after rescuing them all and now you escape first...."

"No, Mummy... never... I will not listen to you and I will never go anywhere without you mummy,...."

Mummy saw his body extremely shivering with great fear but there was no pity on mummy's face. mummy insisted again,

"You must have to listen to me."

Soon after, mummy grabbed John by her arm and tried to lock him inside the bag and John couldn't move before mummy's strength even a little.

But mummy again opened and took John up and made her close to her heart with a harmful kiss on his forehead, it made John a little irritated.

"I never want to leave you, baby,... down,...Not down to life but that life from death,..... and I will always be with you wherever you are,.... just behind as your sweet mummy,......ever,... Sorry dear, I love you so much,..."

Mummy's heart was broken forever, John realized but now mummy stopped her crying and hid his eyes with her hand, and closed the bag.

"Mummy,...No,... Never,... Please,..."

John knocked forcefully from inside the bag.

It was completely dark inside the bag and he could not see anything, only the sound of screaming.

John yelled at Mummy from inside the bag,

" Mummy I am scared,.... mummy come you too,... I cannot live without you...."

It is only now that John begins to realize the severity of the accident but answers don't come because it is really what he expected.

John said, at last,

" I love you, mummy,... I love you so my sweety,..."

Soon he stepped into something else that would break his voice.

At last, he realized mummy had thrown him out and he began to feel breathlessness. It was an extremely terrible condition, his ears were hurt by the strong sound of the wind all around him.

John knew that if he fell down so fast he would surely scatter but he could not do anything only he was able to scream in the throes of death.

In a very short time, John could see the bag going somewhere, hitting and moving and John was so happy to see the branch of trees strike into the bag because he realized that he had landed safely on earth.

Some of the piercing horns made small cuts on his body but John covered his eyes with his hand to prevent the piercing from penetrating his eye.

He was convinced that the bag had hit and stopped somewhere and soon realized that he was now under a regime ruled by silence.

A few sounds came to his ears, passing through the silence in a low voice from his surroundings, but it was all strange to him.

The only sound he could hear was the sound of beetles still resisting the silence, he could hear it regularly when he was at home, but back then he was not attracted to any of it, and now it is the only relief he has here.

"Yes I have landed safely, " John said in his mind but he could not move because something very big fell on him and he could not move under the weight.

It was dark all around and nothing could be seen. He was very weak and lay motionless under it.

Just then, John noticed a torn part of the bag and he looked out through that part.

He was shocked and realized that something strange was going on around him and it was a deep night.

John was terrified when he heard suppressed noises in the silence.

But he did not have to stay in fear for long before that, sleep had closed his eyes.

CHAPTER THREE

John slowly opened his eyes from the knots of sleep. John was lying in a room now, he woke up and looked around in amazement but he didn't understand anything.

John got up from bed and walked on to the next room where he could hear daddy's and mummy's talks and he slowly opened the door and looked suspiciously inside.

His eyes opened unbelievably and the whole room was lit by a table light in that dim light, he can see his daddy and mummy speaking to each other.

But they soon found John, who was hiding.

When they saw John looking suspiciously and called him too. But suddenly he hides in his room again without believing anything that is going on around him.

"Hello nice good morning sweetie,..Why are you hiding there,...? Come here...."

So he heard Daddy's talk for the first time.

While hearing this, a shiver of lightning speed flashed throughout his whole body and then disappeared.

Quickly John ran and leaned toward his mummy and filled his mummy with his kisses.

"Mummy I love you, and where have you been all this time....? I cried when I was without you."

But mummy did not answer anything to crying John.

"So John,... Don't you love me...?" Daddy asked John with suspicion and John saw as his daddy's eyes were filled too.

"Yes daddy... sure I love you too,"...

John jumped from mummy to daddy.

Daddy grabbed John tightly and John could not hold his own against daddy's strength. John saw a plane that had crashed behind daddy. But it was " just a toy" and its body bore the same letter he had previously read from the body of an "Unknown plane."

"Daddy,. I cannot breathe at all,.. Daddy please leave me,...."

This is not what John was supposed to say but it came out of his mouth unawarely because daddy pressed John so much. John tried to push daddy away from him but daddy didn't move and the more he pushed away, the closer it got to himself and again.

His eyes opened because of that discomfort and he realized that he was in the big bag and something heavy was pressing above him.

He took all his might and knocked it off.

Now John can breathe, John realized with great distress that all he had been seeing for so long was just a hollow dream.

"Everything I had seen so far was just a dream but the only one mistake was about my dream because my daddy would never cry. So, I knew right away that this dream could never be believed."

Memories of yesterday's unexpected passing went through his mind again, he couldn't do anything but cry over the events of yesterday.

He wanted so much to stay at home and didn't want to go out to see daddy because when he went out to see daddy once,... It was all unexpected.

Wetness spread all over his eyes, it then flowed towards the cheek but it did not bother John because he saw something that was very disturbing. John looked out again through the same hole in the bag as he looked at last night.

light peered at John through the bag's torn hole. John felt a little relieved because it was a nice morning.

John recalled mummy's words yesterday, as mummy said and pulled up the rope from inside and opened the zip of the bag quickly. Soon the sunshine fell on John's eyes with small force but till now he only half opened and then John shut the bag hard. Because now he saw the very strange place John had never seen before and he was so frightened by the sight of that moment.

"Where am I now,......?"

"Is this the forest anymore,.....?"

"Oops,... Oh my God,...mummy has said that there are animals in the forest that scare children,... Mummy,... I'm scared,...."

John said in a hushed voice.

Suddenly John gets shocked to hear something growling but at the same time, he has realized that the sound was from his stomach.

He gestured to the hungry crying stomach to shut up but it didn't comply.

"No matter how hungry I am, I will not go out until my mummy comes," he said to himself.

But time continued slowly and mummy didn't come after waiting for any length of time, forcing his hunger to get him out.

However, John was careful not to go out due to the fear but nothing could control John and there was no other way to quench his anger without going outside.

Slowly he opened the zip in the bag with a trembling hand. He raised his head a little from inside the bag and looked at the forest carefully.

And he felt as if the forest was so brutal that even in light the darkness is obscured and the danger waits patiently for any good opportunity.

"Anything can happen at any moment without even expecting it" John murmured.

John came out of the bag completely, Soon the forest changed in a big way, the trees suddenly shaken, the sound of wings beating heard above his head. Something follows behind him to pick him up and fly away.

Suddenly he turned back and saw birds flying over his head just as touched and John heard many strange voices that he had never heard before in his life.

John stepped forward holding his hungry stomach.

Unexpectedly a question struck John in his mind,

"What will I eat,.....?"

Because this is not his house, if he was at home, he would have something in the fridge but where can he get food in the forest,... Not forest, in this deadliest forest.

John is now unable to move forward because he is dizzy and felt like he was losing all his control. Somehow the difficulty John reached near the bag again.

There has never been a situation like this in his life. John was convinced that he was experiencing this because he was not eaten.

John was very exhausted and came close to the bag and sat near it.

His eyes stared at the wild forest in his surroundings slowly and the memories of being at home came to his mind. When he was at home he would cry to his mummy for not eating but now he longs for that old food that was refused before.

John patted the nearby bag with love and said,

" It was the bag we brought with mummy" and he remembered the last time he went shopping with mummy.

"Aromatic memories"

Suddenly John jumped up as if remembering something very important.

That was,... he had kept some sweet candy for daddy yesterday in the side compartment of the bag and he must have wanted to fill his stomach even though he had eaten it.

But there was still some doubt in his mind because he was sure that it was not the smell of the chocolates he had reserved for his daddy but the smell of some other fresh chocolates.

John opened the bag without long.

looking up, he was shocked because of the chocolate and food that mummy had wrapped in the big bag.

John recalled that mummy had already reserved everything for him yesterday even during the time of the accident.

He wiped the tears from his eyes and filled his stomach with chocolates.

Probably because of eating chocolates he felt pain in his stomach and unbearable thirst.

John quickly searched for water inside the bag and he was surprised because water is also stored in the bottle in one part of the bag.

Suddenly John was terrified by a frightening noise behind him and quickly climbed into the bag and closed it by pulling the rope and he searched through the torn hole to find out what it was but found nothing there.

" I might have felt that way sometime" John murmured.

But he refused to fully agree with his statement because his mind was telling him that there would be an animal patiently hidden between the plants to catch him when he got out, so he didn't open his bag.

However, John decided to wait until he saw the creature but John did not have to wait long before he fell asleep.

The long sleep of John was disturbed by many amazing voices around him and he opened the bag and looked out to see what the sound was,

He wondered, "The beautiful nature",

The light touched the forest very slowly and the sound of birds he had never heard before and he was so surprised that all this was captured in his sight.

But soon, his mind realized something, a question broke his mind.

"Where is my sweet mummy? "

As usual, tears welled up in his eyes, he saw nothing around him, only the trees and plants that remained silent without answering his question.

However, he did not give up. He walked, ran, wandered, screamed, and longed for a reply from mummy but to no avail.

But,... His screams disturbed the forest and strange sounds came from all around him like grants, shouting and the sound of birds fluttering above his head. As if something was trying to run and draw closer to him, the cruelty of the terrible forest began to be witnessed by the sunlight.

" I am in a big forest now," whispered his mind in horror.

The quiet Jungle is now uneasy and swayed by fear of the arrival of something. His courage melted away from the changes into the forest which had begun to show discomfort from silence, and he looked at nothing else, quickly got into the bag and closed it.

He looked out with his little eyes, winked, looked all around, and saw nothing but the darkness was hidden among the leaves.

After making sure there was nothing around him john slowly stepped out, now all the courage had been drained away and he was very brave when he was inside the bag but the desire to see his mummy made him brave.

He was very tired of the question of where his mummy would be in this big forest?

He looked up at the sky and whimpered,

"When will mummy come,....? I want to see you,"

"Don't cry sweetie,..." He must have been very eager to hear this reply but he knows well that he won't hear it now.

It seems as if they have seen a very beautiful baby crying in the middle of the Jungle, even those woods were still for a moment.

John asked his eyes to calm for a moment. He turned back to the bag that mummy had last given him and he picked up every toy that mummy had given him as a surprise before that made his eyes restless.

Many toys such as cars, bikes, houses, trains, and elephants a lot of, his eyes which had been trying to calm down, were now beginning to become violent. However, John was trained of unexpected changes around him.

John picked up each toy and began to play in the meaning that I was not afraid to take to the scary forest. He acted as if he was happy but when he heard something unexpected sound coming from behind, he ran and hid inside the bag.

John slowly loosened his grip on the bundles of sleep and realized that it was morning.

"Mummy will be there by right now,...?"

He begged God to see his mummy as soon as he opened the bag, and he was assured for no particular reason that "mummy is waiting outside."

So he opened the bag with the great curiosity and looked out, realizing that his hopes had been dashed in an instant, yet the expectations had not faded from his mind, he got out of the bag and searched for his surrounding for mummy and while searching he notice the toys scattered below and remembered yesterday's incident so he was so scared of yesterday that he was afraid to make more noise.

He started playing by picking up each of the toys lying on the floor. John was a little overjoyed and began to put his favorite names on each of his toys and tell them all about his troubles.

But he was still only halfway open his bag, and in the meantime, he was extremely surprised to see what he did not know about. He was eager to see the surprises still left in the big bag for him.

But the sights inside the bag made him very uncomfortable. Looking up at the sky, he asked, without anyone,

"Mummy,... When are you coming,....? I want to see you now," he said.

His sobbing sobs made the whole forest bow their heads and the forest was as quiet as a partner in that little boy's grief.

The birds did not make a sound, nor did they hear the sound of the wind blowing. There was only his moaning in pain.

Inside were his favorite gifts that Mummy was going to give him as a surprise. In none of these did he feel complete happiness, and more than half was lost because he would always look at his mummy's face when she gave him a present.

He must have longed to see the face that echoed that love because mummy's gifts are close but mummy is still far away.

Toys, shirts, books, watches, and so on,... It may have been that mummy had bought all this earlier without informing him.

"No,... Never,... My mummy will come soon, and I'm sure it'll hurt her if I cry."

He once again remembered mummy's last words in his mind just before he left her,

"I'll always be behind you, I'm sure."

The mummy's words that once sounded in his mind were so comforting to him, and soon he was filled with Joy and expectations without reason.

He picked up every toy his mummy had bought for him and began to play. Cars, bikes, elephants, horses, houses, and so on...

His joy knew no bounds. He spent time playing and giving his favorite toys his favorite names. He knows very well how to push the time forward in times when mummy is not around because the times around mummy are the only most precious times and moments he knows.

Inside the vast jungle where the face of the mystery is mysteriously hidden,Gradually, without even realizing it. Soon a baby's laugh spread across the forest which quickly spread to every direction in the forest.

"John didn't realize that the wild animals that had begun to taste human flesh were dozing off in this big forest."

The light is trying to disappear into the darkness, and a little darkness is beginning to spread in the sky.

He returned from his long-drawn-out game to the strangeness and raised his eyes to the sky, perhaps it was because the surroundings seemed so strange to him that the doll fell from his hand.

He was horrified to see the darkness touching the woods, and immediately he climbed into the big bag that he felt was a refuge.

His eyes were filled with the horrible sight of his aging grandparents burning before him at the time of the accident, and occasionally the luggage fell so hard on the heads of the passengers due to the unexpected shaking on the flight that very few people managed to overcome it and the others had to end their efforts there.

The horrible situation all around,... the sound of alarm piercing through the ear, red light that hurts the eyes. Because of all this, his body was not alive, he had already died seeing the horrible sights going on around him but one question remained in him because there was no one near him.

"Where is my mummy,.....?" But by then Mummy had picked him up.

"Yes,...That's right, I hadn't seen Mummy up close for a while before the flight crashed.

So Mummy planned to put all the food and water that I needed for my survival into this bag.

In fact, My mummy was really leading me to life when expecting life to no longer exist and to be defeated in the face of death, even in the midst of others dying."

He wiped away the tears from top to bottom.

"I know my mummy is an intelligent person so my mummy will come anyway and I will see mummy,.. it sure."

But time went on, John played and sang and danced and moved the time forward because he knows very well how to move time forward when there is no mummy with him.

After a while, his stomach started to get irritated. John went to the bag and opened the chocolate covers he had broken yesterday, but he couldn't bear the sights because the ants were wrapped in the chocolate covers.

Suddenly, filled with anger, John crushed and beat ants approaching the chocolate cover again and again.

He threw all the chocolate wrapped by ants into the woods in extreme anger.

Yet an angry restless John, weeping like screaming, told anyone of his grievances.

But John still didn't realize that he had thrown half of his whole food Into the Woods.

John took the good chocolates that the ant didn't sift and put them away safely. John was troubled by the pain of losing so many chocolates and wiping away his tears and trying to contain his worries.

While eating, John kept some of the good chocolates in a special package to give to Mummy, When mummy comes.

"Because mummy will be very hungry anyway when mummy arrives. So mummy will be very happy when I give her chocolates," John said and looked at those chocolates which were separated for his mummy.

Darkness spread into the atmosphere as if to forget the light. The sound of birds fluttering their wings and the roar of other beasts frightened him greatly. Something was flying above him and something was running behind him, he was totally scared.

Suddenly he got into the bag and he ran his eyes out through the hole in the bag but John could not see anything terrible there outside because the forest was still not awake.

"I need to sleep before the forest wakes up," John told him unknowingly, because he had understood the cruelty of the forest in recent days.

John turned and stopped looking outside. A lot of thoughts went through his little mind and it was all worrying him, and tears must have crossed his soft cheeks to remember something.

John asked himself,

"How many days have I not seen my mummy now?"

"How happy I was when I was with my mummy. I just need to go to my mummy, not wanting chocolates and cakes."

Memories of being at home with mummy made John cry and suddenly Donna's face came into his mind.

"What would she do now,..? Sometimes she is asleep now and anyway it is better to be a beggar like her than to live like this,... and I don't want to be Donna's husband........ As mummy said, just be her brother, then I can always stay with my mummy and I don't want to be a detective officer. I just need to get home with mummy somehow."

By this time his voice had risen without his knowledge.

His groans inside the bag may have attracted the cruel animal outside because the other face of the forest was yet to be seen.

Like a warning, it woke John up because of the strange noises he heard around the bag. John listened intently to the many sounds he heard outside to see if they were the sound he had heard before, but none were familiar to him, As if distracting him from his attention he was unknowingly being attacked by sleep.

John woke up from his sleep to an unexpected sound and as soon as he got up, he was intrigued by the suspicion that it was mummy, because there is someone outside who is breathing like his mummy, so someone waiting for him outside, sure.

"Maybe it is my mummy,......?"

For a moment Joy flew through his mind at lightning speed. John raised his hand to unzip the bag and gave up his attempt with slight hesitation.

"Wouldn't she talk to me if she was my mummy?"

Soon he Peered out through the old hole in the bag.

For the first moment, he saw nothing but in the dim light of the moon he saw a creature's footsteps approaching his bag and the cruelty had its eyes gleaming even in the dark.

"Something very terrible beast"

His body froze for a moment when he saw that beast but John regained his composure and quickly closed the hole the beast came on the top of the bag and hit it hard and tried to tear it apart, which scared him a lot because the bag might have collapsed during the attack.

After a long struggle, everything calmed down and the creature seemed to be gone, now John was relieved.

But John didn't dare to open the bag, so he looked through the hole again to clear his doubts but this time John was really caught and the creature didn't go away.

Unfortunately, it saw him Looking through the hole from a distance then it quickly ran closer to him,......

The excitement of finding the prey is shining in its eyes, and it's running swiftly towards John.

CHAPTER FOUR

John was convinced that the creature was now standing outside the bag. John knew that his heartbeat and breathing were so loud that the creature could easily understand it. John can suppress anything else but he can never do both.

The creature is still standing there making frightening noises.

After a while, he had not heard any sound of the creature, but he covered his mouth so that not a trace of noise would come out of him.

At the end of the continuous effort of the creature for such a long time John realized that the creature cannot break his bag and come in anyway, so John wanted to look again to make sure the creature was gone but now he saw something in the crack which was trying to get inside.

By seeing this, John was a little scared but later confirmed that it was the creature's nose because daddy had told John earlier that animals could recognize humans by smell.

John thought he could pick up any one of the clothes lying nearby and throw it at it, but he didn't do that and immediately took the bottle of water in front of his eyes and poured it forcefully into the creature's nose.

The water rushed into its nostrils and It began to sneeze and spit so loudly that it ran into the forest.

Then for a while, John heard no sound of the creature but lay motionless to confirm that there was no hint of that cruel beast.

John was relieved now that he had a smile and appreciated himself for his intelligent action and started talking about himself without any more,

"At first I thought I could throw my dress against its nose but I didn't do it, because my dress would have the smell of my body on it. Daddy has said that animals find humans based on their smell so my dress will definitely have my smell so it can easily find me and then the dress will bite through the small hole and try to pull it out, then the bag will tear more than the old size of hole and can be easily caught me up.

"But,...But how can my smell recognize it if the water goes on its nose....? I noticed when I had a fever that I couldn't smell anything which meant that if water went through its nose, it couldn't smell anything. That is why I decided to do that."

John felt an indescribable joy as he used his little intellect to prevent the great danger from coming.

He changed away from the place where the water fell and lay down but still, the fear did not set him free.

Even though, for a moment he remembered his mummy and closed his little eyes.

A good morning,.... the sunlight has crept through the bag. Even then, darkness was hidden in the wilds of the woods. John slowly opened his eyes and simply wished that, "it was enough to be my home"

" Will my mummy come today?" John was questioned inside.

"It was enough to come, if I was at home, how beautiful it was in the morning and It is better to get up in the morning and go to school than to lie in the forest alone."

" If I didn't wake up early in the morning, mummy would come up and get up and fight with me, sometimes she would beat me and I was worried all those days but no matter how much I get today, it is all right to go home."

John slowly unzipped the bag and then looked outside.

" I am still in the woods and my mummy has not come yet,...." the answer hid his smile.

He went out into the woods and unzipped his pants for preparations for urination and started.

But,.... suddenly a memory flashed through his mind and he ran towards the bag without urinating completely and sat inside the bag.

"Could that beast that came yesterday still be gone from here now? Or will it still be hiding in the forest to catch me....?"

John said in his mind as he looked into the woods through the crack in the bag. It seemed to John that the trees and plants swaying in the wind might have meant, "maybe"

"If so, shouldn't that animal scare my mummy too...? I need to see my mummy as soon as possible and should tell mummy that there is an animal here that scares the little children." John made up his mind.

"Anyway I can find my mummy and I will try my best and then go home as soon as possible,.... or if I do not see my mummy one day, I can come back here and then next morning I look for mummy again and I will continue to do this until I see mummy."

Something John had planned in his little mind. John was willing to open that bag even though fear was holding him back, he opened the bag and looked up, making sure there was nothing. There is only a forest around him so he has no idea where to go,...

" Front,.. back,... left,...and right. today I will go ahead and go back tomorrow" So he thought he could find his mummy in just four days and it made him very excited.

But by then John had been devastated by the sight and most of the new big bag he and his mummy had shopped at the last moments had been torn apart by the creature's attack.

John was paid special attention to mummy's face when she brought this bag, what a joy on that beautiful face,

"My favorite mummy,...."

Those memories of the last time she shopped with his mummy went through his mind a little emotionally.

"My dear mummy,... I love you so much ever,...."

While staring helplessly at the torn bag, John noticed something. A letter lying in the outer compartment of the bag caught his eyes.

John was very anxious and picked up the letter in his hand. It was so beautifully wrapped up and has a mind-pleasing aroma, this was all he could understand and there was also a small note on the outside of the letter cover.

"To my dear husband "

He read those letters effortlessly.

"Oh,... this is a letter that mummy wrote to give to my daddy,... What would this letter have been written for,....? Isn't this a letter to daddy,......?Would mummy be upset if I opened it and read it,....?

I will,......No,... I won't read this letter and keep it in my hand until I see daddy and I will give it to my daddy safely,...."

"I need to take care of something when I go looking for Mummy, I need to fill this little bag with all food, water and also needed clothes. It was my daddy Who taught me this when I was trekking with my daddy before." John advised himself.

There was also a small bag of John's in that big bag. In that little bag, John put all the things he wanted.

Chocolates, water bottles, a few toys, and so on,... In the meantime, his eyes fell on the book that,

"Mummy brought it for me at the last moment," John murmured.

"If only I'd had those moments of buying this book once more I would tell my mummy not to come on this flight"

John bowed his head as if he were an unlucky man and he took the book out of his big bag and read the letters on the top of the book,

"AKID UNDER THE TWO WOLVES"

He remembered that he had been with Mummy when he read the same words before. Then he put the book in his bag without wanting to see it anymore.

John filled the little bag with everything he needed and all the things were taken out again from the bag to make sure everything was taken because before going to school his mummy would tell him that he had to make sure he had all the books have taken or else he'd have to worry later.

John took the bag and started walking forward and after walking a little he looked back.

Sometimes he might have thought about his mummy but he saw nothing there beyond trees and plants.

He said goodbye to them though he had a burning sadness in his mind and was not ready to show off.

"Maybe I will be back in the evening because I need to find mummy somehow and,... I'll go back home after I find my mummy and I will be back to see you all again before I go back,...."

In such a short time he had made them his own friends and raised his hand and said as if swearing,

"I will search the whole forest for mummy until I see mummy again"

John is also very upset about leaving his friends, but he must have gone to find mummy anyway.

Finally, John came closer to that torn bag again and some of the memories again made him very sad.

John gave a cute kiss to the torn bag and said,

"Don't worry, once I see mummy, I will only go back with you and I will never leave you in this Woods and,... Yes...I know,..... sure,... I will show Mummy the wounds you had yesterday."

After a silence, he again continued,...

"I know you're hurting now, but you are not crying,...but, Do you know how many times I have cried today,...?"

John said in a stumbling voice. Then, he turned and walked away without looking at anything.

"It would have been enough to have Billy with me. If I had him I would not be alone now." He remembered Billy.

Billy is the only one cute cat in his house and he loved Billy very much but mummy won't let to take the cat with him when he goes to daddy on the flight but John loved it so much that his mummy sent it to his friend's house several days earlier so that he wouldn't cry when he had to part ways and mummy consoled John by saying that she will bring it later.

"Mummy is very intelligent,..... but Kevin always touches it and loses its cuteness. They told mummy that they'd take care of Billy like gold but let us go back and see how Billy looks like ".

John continued to walk, and he'd forgotten between his thoughts that the big bag was getting away from him.

Large trees and plants crowded around him as if welcoming him and John stepped forward to dispel the darkness hidden by the leaves with his light.

John entered the heart of the forest. Behind the wildness, horror, and danger of the forest hidden like a murderer and the sound around him did not frighten him with a strangeness because his only one aim was to see his mummy somehow.

He stood there as if he had suddenly remembered something as he walked away,

"I didn't eat anything this morning, I forgot to eat in a hurry to go, and mummy would definitely scold me if I didn't eat breakfast."

"I am really sorry mummy,... I won't repeat this mistake anymore."

He said with a heartbreaking pain because mummy's words were the only thing that always stuck in his mind during this time when mummy was not close to him.

If he's been away from his mummy's words now, it is like John's been away from his mummy forever.

John sat down under a nearby big tree and quickly opened the bag and began to greedily pick up all the sweets he liked and ate them but he didn't like to eat chocolates in the morning but the hunger forced him to eat more.

But he could not eat anymore and as his stomach ached, John stopped eating and still did not forget to set aside mummy's chocolates.

After drinking the water, John decided to rest here for a while.

"Daddy will say that when we go trekking,... he tells me to eat and take a rest for a while,... I usually sit on top of

Daddy while traveling and mummy takes water, food, and clothes but now I have to take everything myself."

After thinking something he again continued,

"Daddy is so funny, he always makes the jokes and makes me laugh"

John unknowingly talks to the trees and plants about his old memories even if there is no one around him.

He says with a smiley face but he is struggling not to be filled with tears.

After a long conversation, John slowly fell into a trance.

His eyes were disturbed by the sunlight falling through the branches of the tree but he still couldn't stop sleeping and his eyes opened and closed occasionally and then returned to sleep. However, the desire in his mind brought him out of his sleep.

"I want to see my mummy soon" before nightfall."

His lips quivered slightly from his sleep... Then, with some difficulty, he opened his eyes wide and looked around anxiously.

"It seems to be evening because it was always at this time that I left school.

In the evening, the teachers don't come to class, and at that time, I would sit in the class and wait for mummy to come out.

In the past, I only needed to wait for a while to see mummy even though I would cry unnecessarily if mummy came a little late. But... Now I don't even know when to see mummy."

Thoughts emanating from his memories made him very upset.

"It doesn't matter if you are worried, let us get up and try to see mummy," John said to himself.

Before getting ready to go, he noticed the chocolate covers he had discarded after eating but he did not want to leave them there alone and he took them and kept them in his bag then continued walking, Brushing with his hand the plant and grasses that stretched above him.

He didn't know where he was going but he began to walk around with the firmness that he was going ahead.

On the way, his hands and legs were cut off by hitting by small sticks and thrown and some insects would bite and hurt him, and that all made him furious with the pain and itching.

He would also try to hit small insects that bite his legs and arms from time to time but they escape before John can see them and start beating them, but the angry John hits them hard enough to kill the insect but they escape adventurously.

But this would upset John a lot because he realized that he was hurting himself by the beating and that no small creatures were dying. He sat there and started crying, he wiped away the tears flowing down his cheeks and continued to cry.

Anyway, He knows very well that no one in this forest is going to see him cry But he cannot stop caring because he has been so annoyed by that situation.

John kept a special look at the wounded part to show when the mummy came. Because when mummy sees his wounds, she will feel sorry for him and love him more but all his patience will be ruined when he sees insects biting him even while crying.

"I think they have the teeth of a dog, what a pain it is to bite, even I cry you cannot leave me alone without biting me?" He appealed to them.

"When I was in school the kids in the class would argue with me and when I finally cried they would stop arguing as well as,...How many times have I cried now?,.... and can you,......? without bothering me like that anymore,....please,.."

Who to listen,... Who understands,... John realized that nothing would ever happen there except the swarm of insects, unable to bear it at all he moved to another place.

He sat under another tree looking up at the sky that was about to darken.

The darkness began to spread all around, John was fully disappointed that he could not see the mummy before nightfall.

"Did my mummy forget about me,...?"

"Doesn't mummy want me anymore,...?"

"Because mummy said while on the flight that, "I love all children equally"

If that is the case, then if the love that loves me loves another child then surely the love for me will vanish, and sometimes mummy's love for me has waned,... "

"If,... if mummy had loved me, Mummy would surely have come to this forest for me,...When mummy showed the same love she showed me to another baby, she forgot about me there and now has another baby in my place,...."

His voice stumbled in the middle of crying.

He struggled not to cry but the tears rushed out forcefully and it gently caressed his soft cheek and then dropped down and disappeared.

His attention was drawn to the surroundings by the unexpected change as if something was trying to follow just behind him and its loud noises and footsteps terrified him a lot.

He was so frightened that he hid among the grass and curiosity waited to know what was coming behind him.

'It was a herd of deer,'

Each of the beautiful deer passed him happily returning to its home.

"Wow,... Dears,....."

"The same deers I saw when I went to the animal park with my mummy,... How cute they are,... They look like my Billy,... "

He watched in amazement as each deer passed by, in that group he especially noticed the walk of a little deer. That little deer is walking very happily with his mummy.

"I used to walk around with my mummy in a very happy way like this before when I went to see my daddy but...." his voice got a little break.

The last deer overtook him. He stared with horseradish eyes until they disappeared Into the woods and only his moaning of being called" MUMMY " was breaking that silence.

"Mummy, I miss you so much,...Where are you,......?"

He could not control himself from crying.

The darkness slowly began to appear and the light began to disappear and everything seemed quiet as if to embrace the darkness into their own kingdom.

John noticed that birds entered its cage for fear of the dark and their sound echoed throughout the area.

"Mother birds might be happy to see their baby birds and the baby birds may be happy to see their mother birds,..." he guessed in his mind.

"They will be very happy to see mummy, which babies who want to be quiet when they see their Mummy,....? I also have a lot to say." John said looking at his injuries.

Suddenly he remembered something, the night is near and he must get to the bag before the night because it will be very difficult to find a way after the nightfall. He grabbed his bag and started running.

John had already decided to walk back the way he came.

Only now did John realize that he was really wrong.

" Which way did I come...?"

This question stunned him for a moment.

He felt as if he was now unfamiliar with the forest he had seen for so long. Doubts arose within him but he refused to give up and he wandered around with the belief that the path he had taken would come to memory again.

For a long time, John wandered in the woods for the way he had come but as he wandered the forest seemed so unexpectedly that he could not find a familiar way.

He was very unfamiliar around him and he could not remember anything even though he had been in this forest for so long.

This was a situation he had never expected, so he felt as if he had lost all hope that was left of him.

As he lost all hope, his running slowed down and the vision of his eyes became blurred. He didn't see the way of expectations to move forward, and soon his footsteps were firmly in a place, unable to leap forward,

Eventually, his whole body becomes exhausted and he can no longer run.

His eyes were seen the darkness harden on the light and the sound of the birds around him began to fade away he watched anxiously as the last bird reached its nest.

"It was enough to not get out of the bag"

He bowed his head down because he was very upset with his own decision but not only sadness but also fear madc John uneasy.

"If any creatures come to attack me during these times they can kill me very easily,.."

He shuddered, the silence of the forest and the power of the darkness closed his eyes. He could do nothing but cry then.

"If only someone had come and saved me."

Vain thoughts and desires made him very upset and the coming of the night is so intense that John now has only the light of the moon shining above his head but he sees the moon's light very dim because it is interrupted by the big trees.

The surrounding trees and the plants are frozen in fear of the dark and they have become like Mere shadows.

John began to hear many sounds of the forest, which he soon began to feel familiar and there was the murmur and howl.

He knows that ferocious beasts and creatures that kill and eat humans come out at night because they can be seen even at night but he cannot,...

"How many street lights are there near my house and could anyone bring some of them here,...?" If I had it, I would have escaped if any wild animal came to attack me at night," John argued with someone out of his childish mind.

Among a group of trees in the woods, he noticed a tree with large roots at its base. John climbed through those roots and found a better place where he can lie down.

" I will try to fall asleep soon or I will be scared more"

He shook his head as if realizing something and he tried to lie down with his little bag like a pillow.

He tried very hard to calm down but he couldn't and he felt as if sleep was drifting away from him,...

"Why did God create this forest....?"

"Maybe to scare the little children,..."

"Where will my mummy be now,...?"

"Would the mummy be afraid to stand alone in this vast forest,.......?"

"Oh,... My poor mummy,...."

A lot of questions that came to his mind prevented him from sleeping.

All the noises coming up to break the silence terrified him so much.

"Mummy,.... mummy,....." he called to himself without realizing it.

The legs and arms were constricted, and the eyelids are pressed firmly so that the eyes do not open unknowingly.

The tears struggled so hard through the tightly closed eyelids that it jumped out and began to reach towards the ear.

The guilt of having lost his old big bag kept attacking him brutally in the darkness without leaving him.

Every single memory haunted him, saddening, frightening,...

Memories of being with mummy,.... Memories of being with the daddy,.... Memories of playing with friends,..... Memories of arguing with the mummy,... Memories of mummy sleeping with him at night,...

Among these, he felt as if he were being dragged away unknowingly through each memory.

It was the horrible memories that frightened him more than the cruel beasts of the night because the cruelty of the cruel animal ends with death, but the cruelty of the cruel memories lasts until he dies.

John longed for sleep because the memories had disturbed him so much and his eyes frightened as if he was sad not by fear, and slowly the sleep kissed him without letting him become sadder.

It's a very beautiful morning, because John is now with his mummy, and every morning he is with mummy is pretty as usual for him, but one question made him very anxious,

Isn't it the day to go to school,...?

Although these thoughts constantly disturbed him, he again covered his head with a blanket so that he could not turn away from his sleep.

From time to time, he removed the blanket over his head and looked at the door of the room as if to know something, because it was at this time that mummy would come in unexpectedly and if he sleeps even when mummy comes, surely mummy will argue or sometimes get punishment.

But none of this had frightened him the most, but mummy would tell daddy every little mistake he made.

But even after daddy knew all this, daddy would never scold or hit John, and daddy would never scold him as mummy scolds him, but the name "good boy" that Daddy calls him is sometimes likely to change because John is always a good boy in front of Daddy and he always wants to stay in it without any change.

He is unknowingly dragged into sleep but comes back to consciousness as if he has remembered something very urgent, but soon he becomes a victim of sleep deprivation that drags him back.

Even in his sleep, he paid special attention to one thing, and it was too late for Mummy to wake him up.

It was only now that he remembered one thing and he awoke happily from his sleep,

"No school today,... Because today is a holiday,.."

Mummy does not bother him during the holidays and it is common to let him sleep again, and it still does.

The discussions that took place in the class yesterday evening about the holiday passed as evidence in his mind. Very soon John fell back into bed but could not sleep so he decided to get up.

If he goes to bed during the holidays, those moments will be lost very quickly because every moment he spends with his mummy is very precious to him.

As he stepped out of bed and walked forward, he turned back as a memory of something returned to his mind, thought of something for a moment, then ran to the window.

The window in his room is taller than him, but with great difficulty, he somehow climbs out and crawls out to look out,

"Daddy,.. where are you now,...?"

But he knows that his question is in vain.

He would look expectantly at the vehicles appearing from a distance, but as the entrance of his house passed, his hopes would be aimed at distances again.

But none of this bothers him because a lot of vehicles pass in front of his house, taking his eyes off the distant vehicles and leaning towards the approaching vehicles.

In the course of his attentive view, he caught sight of someone walking from far away, and he could be sure of one thing, even if it was a distant sight, that person would be a powerful muscle man anyway, but there was nothing special to look forward to because so many people were still passing in front of his eyes.

Unexpectedly by then, unknowingly his legs moved down as if to slip and fall, but with the help of the window, he prevented himself from falling and jumped down.

Even if it was an unexpected accident, it didn't scare him very much because this accident was not the first time he had faced this accident that many times he had encountered it.

He descended from his room through the stairs to the down floor,

and crawled up the sofa.

"Mummy,... Good morning..."

"Oh yeah,... Very good morning my sweetheart "

He might have liked his mummy's response very much because a smile quickly flashed on his face.

As usual, his gaze fell on the clock, and his smile soon began to fade.

"If there was school today, these were the moments when I would have prepared to go to school with great difficulty"

But he had not had time to think about it for a long time and before that he had heard a voice and his attention had been distracted.

Treeeeering,... Treeeeeeing,...

It was the sound of a bell ringing and his eyes suddenly fell on the outer door of the house.

"Mummy,... someone is waiting outside for you."

He heard his mummy's words in a low voice from inside,

"John, I'm very busy so you can see who it is."

But this one answer of mummy's was never something he had ever expected because mummy never let John open the door when strangers came home. No matter how busy mummy is, only mummy opens the door.

He walked to the door, unable to make sense of his mummy's sudden change now.

Somehow he opened the door, though with some difficulty. But what he saw was very unexpected,

A stranger.....

However, turned the stranger's face so that John couldn't see and John was sure it was the same person he'd seen from a distance when he looked up from above.

But even after he arrives, the stranger does not speak to him and the stranger's strong arms and body disturbed his voice,

"Hello,... Good... morning uncle,...What do you want,...?"

"I want John. I saw a very handsome little boy looking at me through the window from above.

I loved him so much that I would never leave here without getting him back."

The stranger's harsh voice frightened John, but one more question remained in his mind,

"Sorry uncle,... Uncle, where did you get my name from,...?"

The stranger's reply came a little late,

"I've been targeting you for a few days, and every time you went to school I would follow you without you knowing, So, I could find your house, ...Anyway, this is my best chance I'll get you out of here very soon,...."

"Mummy,... Help meeeee"

Even before his cry could be heard, the stranger turned towards John.

Seeing the stranger, his eyes widened in amazement,

Daddy,..... Were you....?

Soon daddy lifted him up,

"My sweetie,... Did you scare,....?

"Yeah,... I always expected only jokes from You,... Daddy."

Soon John clung to Daddy's heart and meanwhile, he saw mummy standing smiling behind daddy.

"Mummy daddy has come,...."

Mummy said to him with a smile,

"I already knew Daddy was coming,..."

The Faint light from the sun slowly Pierced his eyes. John forcibly opened his eyes and looked around.

"Is it morning,......?So quickly,......"

John felt as if the trees and plants around him had nodded "yes" at his question.

And now he can feel very happy because, what now comforts him is the single hope that he will be able to regain his all hopes, which he had previously lost, by the shelter of light.

"Today I'll find mummy anyway and I'll find my missing bag, too,..."

He took a long breath in and then he became aware of each of the goals he has set for himself today.

John slowly picked up the bag and slowly descended from the foot of the very large rooted tree where he had been lying yesterday.

He turned around a little awkwardly and looked at the big tree and said "thanks" and then hid In the woods.

On the way, he picked up a stick lying on the ground and held it in his hand.

"If any creatures come to frighten me,

I will show them the stick and frighten them."

He said a little angrily and he named the little stick "Mickey" then he continued his journey by knocking down the plant in front of him with his Mickey.

During the walk ahead he saw very colorful butterflies in his sight and he was very surprised because this is the first time he saw such butterflies and watched very carefully as butterflies full of many colors drinking honey and playing and flying around together happily.

"I used to enjoy playing with my friends regularly,...How beautiful were the days with them? But now there is no one with me,..."

The memories of playing with his friends made him very depressed.

One of the butterflies hit John on his forehead and fell down and he noticed it.

He bent down to pick up the fallen butterfly but he found it with great difficulty, as the place where he was treading was full of dry leaves and he laid it in the palm of his hand.

"Wow,... beautiful one...."

John gently touched its wings with his finger and the colored dust from it stuck to his fingers and it made him very anxious, but as if suddenly remembering something, it got up and flew away. John was a little upset but he didn't cry because the tears seemed to have disappeared by last night and what's still left is to cry in the coming days.

John ignored it and walked on.

During the journey, he realized that his stomach was trying to tell him something and from there he opened the bag and took the chocolates in his hand and also he did not forget to set aside what mummy needed even though he is so hungry.

The journey continued with eating chocolates because there was no time to waste.

Mummy and the bag had to be found before nightfall, and his decision was reaffirmed again.

After eating, the chocolate covers were kept separate without throwing them out. John quickly gathered for the walk. He still had bruises on his arms and legs and the insects were bothering him but John was not bothered because he was adapted to the forest.

However, his goal was to see the mummy because he had adapted to his mummy since he was born.

CHAPTER FIVE

A boy passes through a dense forest, his goal is to see his mummy, but perhaps because he is not familiar with this forest, he walks with great difficulty. There must have been a place around him that he had never seen before, and a little fear was drawn on his innocent face.

The sounds of birds and the chirping of beetles follow him along the way. He is never going to be alone in this big forest, many who see him are hiding in this forest and it seems that they are trying to talk to him but he does not know how to answer them?

Because he was so small, the views around him were obscure, but he would occasionally try to see the heights by jumping, but it would not be of much use to him because he did not know where to go and it was his first experience of living with this forest without being anyone.

Maybe it's because he's hoping someone's around him somewhere around him that he's trying to ask someone out loud for help,

"Uncle,... aunty,... Is anyone here,...?"

He asked in a loud voice, but even though his voice was reflected in his surroundings, there were no answers from anywhere.

His voice spread slightly in that great forest, and the birds heard his voice and flew up into the sky as if frightened, and there was silence around as if all were listening to his high-pitched voice. running and walking, his question continued again and again, but he could find no answer from anywhere but to hear his voice reflected.

It was then that he noticed that the surrounding plants were trying to hide something from him. He ran to those herds of plants.

As he ran, he began to see clearly the sky hidden by the plants, and as the distant sky approached his vision, the more he began to feel the lost hope and saw the sight through the bushes that obstructed his vision.

His eyes sparkled with amazement, and the breeze touched his face and passed by.

As he had expected, he is now on a mountain, and he can see the valley and the big trees standing tall in the distance.

He looked very carefully at the slopes and valleys of the hills, hoping that he would be able to see the humans or their houses or their vehicles from this height.

But even after a long time, he was unable to rely on his expectations because it was the huge trees that stood in the way of him, mainly preventing him from seeing distant sights.

He realized that the same tall trees he saw in the distance were still near him, So how could he see very small men under the tall trees that far away?

"Sometimes they'll be under the big trees in the distance, just like me... Because of the tall trees, they may not be able to see the high sights, and,... maybe somewhere there is my mummy looking for me like this?"

"Mummy,... Can you hear me,....? I'm here, your sweetie,... I love you so much,...... Mummy,..."

He knows that his voice will never go too far, but he is unwittingly compelled to do so by the intensity of his desires.

At last, he became so tired that not a single sound came out of his throat, but he wiped away the tears that flowed across the boundaries.

He was leaning against a tree that was leaning against the valley next to him. There is still a long way to go to find Mummy, but the hope that one day he will be able to find Mummy put a smile on his face, but it did not last long.

John is following Daddy, carrying a small bag, and there's mummy just behind him.

"Mummy,.. hurry up, we have to overtake Daddy."

But mummy, who was carrying too much weight behind him, smiled and looked at him in the sense that 'she couldn't'.

Daddy too carries a lot of weight but daddy is not like mummy because daddy is a 'powerful muscle man' and daddy can lift mummy but mummy can never lift daddy.

"Daddy,... I'm so tired, I cannot move forward anymore." But before John could stop, Daddy put him on Daddy's shoulder.

"Did my sweetie get tired so quickly?"

"Yes Daddy,... I'm so tired." He said with a little embarrassment.

John, who was sitting on top of Daddy, can now see the distant views more clearly than before.

Pointing to something farther away, and he asked,

"What's that daddy,...?

"That's the lighthouse, and if someone is stuck somewhere while trucking in this big forest, the lighthouse helps them understand direction and not go astray.If someone goes astray, just follow the direction in which the lighthouse sees it and where they will get help anyway......When night falls, that big house will light up and that's why it's called the lighthouse,.."

John muttered as if he'd learned something from Daddy's answers.

"Yes,... Daddy, you are right,.... "

There were only huge forests around but he kept moving forward. He walks with great difficulty through the large bushes that are taller than him, and he endures itching, pain, and swelling while walking, but he has begun to adapt to it all with great difficulty.

He endured the face of the cruelty of the jungle, without even being considered a child.

The sight he saw from the top of the mountain had raised great expectations in him, and it would certainly be evidence of human habitation,.. of course.

"Get there as soon as possible, ask someone for help, escape from this dense jungle and find mummy, then..live happily with mummy."

The desires that were increasing day by day in him created expectations and those expectations forced him into his desire.

When he feels hungry during the journey, he will sit under a tree and take the chocolates out of the bag.

After resting for a while, the journey will resume. Aiming for a hope he had seen in the valley.

Eventually, he realized that it was very close to the same place he had seen from the top of the hill, and this was a road just like he had thought before.

He waited there for some time with desires and hopes, for the arrival of any vehicle, and soon a vehicle he had seen before in the distance caught his eye.

He saw the vehicle from a distance and the boundless joy went beyond the boundaries of his mind because there would definitely be humans in that vehicle and if he asked them he would surely be able to escape and find Mummy.

The car stopped next to him.

"Hello uncle,... Can you stop the car,..? please,.. "

"Yes of course,..."

He had climbed into the vehicle without looking at anything else, but he had forgotten to see the place where it was getting dark for the last time in his overwhelming pleasure.

It was the same experience as going in the car with his mummy before and soon that realization made his eyes a little wet.

As he was traveling in the vehicle, he tried to talk to that stranger,

"Uncle,... Can you help me,...? I'm very sad now because I lost my mummy a few days ago,..."

While he was saying this, he tried his best not to cry but he could not.

"Yes John,... I can understand the sadness in your mind and definitely, I will help you then,.......I have seen your mummy before.... Therefore I will take you to your mummy as soon as possible."

But John was not relieved by the stranger's favorable words, and he could now understand better, and what was going on in him now, with skepticism, even though, John asked the stranger again,

"Sorry uncle,... I haven't told you my name yet, then,... How did you know my name?.."

But he really didn't need a stranger's answer to understand what was going on around him.

During the walk, he saw something and his speed slowed down and he still had to walk along a light path but that road was also blocked by a large tree branch and It had lost all its leaves and only its horns remained.

He looked up to see where this large branch had fallen from and saw that the top of a nearby tree had completely fallen off.

In the meanwhile, he can see a way too, and immediately he walked down that narrow path.

While entering, He covered his eyes and face to prevent the piercing of small horns.

As a result, the other side of his hidden wrist began to cut slightly.

The repeated piercing of the horns into the wound hurt him so much and also he could not see clearly the obstacles in front of him as his eyes were covered with his hands.

But he refused to change his covered hands because he knows the wound on his hands is still in excruciating pain but the slightest horn piercing into his eye is something he can't even imagine because it's so scary, even when he thinks about it.

He heard something unexpected sound coming from between the tree branches,

Krrrrr,... rrreee,......

Immediately he looked back with a shock.

The tree branches pierced and a small part of his bag was torn. He tried to pull out a piece of stick that had been stabbed but that attempt again created more cracks.

His heart ached so much because of his one moment's carelessness that the bag was torn because this little bag was the surprise gift his mummy had bought for the last time.

Eventually, he came out of the tree branches with great difficulty, he had scratches on his hands and feet due to the tree branches but it did not bother him much but the scratches on the bag were the most frustrating to him.

But very soon he heard a loud noise and a tremor passed through his body at lightning speed. He looked up at the sky and even the sky was obscured by his view because of the big trees that stood tall.

However, he realized that it was going to rain, but before he knew it, drops had fallen on his face, overtaking the branches of a large tree.

He ran off in search of a safe place to avoid getting wet, but by then his body was almost half wet.

At last, he leaned closer to a tree.

Now he feels a little relieved from the rain but not more.

"If mummy sees me wet in the rain, she will definitely scold me."

Before he could finish his words, his tears and the raindrops mingled with each other.

A spacious playground, where some children were playing happily and their laughter was beginning to warm the surroundings.

But the sudden changes in the sky and thunder and lightning became a hindrance to their happiness.

The sky was full of black clouds and unexpectedly passing thunder but it did not frighten them but the fear that Mummy would quarrel if they played in the rain kept them away from their immersive games.

All the children who were playing hid under a nearby tree because of the rain but only one child was immersed in the game again and again and the fear did not deter him.

"Hey John,... come here,... Mummy will argue with you if you play in the rain." A boy in the group called out to him.

He turned back very impressively, with an affectionate smile because he was such a handsome little guy.

Soon after dropping the bat in his hand, he too ran towards them and his wet lips whispered,

"Hey,... Even if we stay here to keep the rain from getting wet, there's not going to be a big deal because we're all already wet with the rain, so mummy will scold us anyway,...."

After a few moments of silence, he again continued,

"Shall we still play in the rain,....?"

They listened to John's words and looked at each other because John was right, by now everyone is completely wet.

There was a smile on their faces as the drops of water seeped down their faces.

"Yes,... Let's go,..."

They continued to play more happily

than before, and the laughter of the children who had vanished despite the pouring rain had begun to spread throughout the atmosphere.

"Bye,... Bye,... See you tomorrow,... "

Everyone said goodbye after the games and returned to their homes

Mummy had seen John from a distance, wet in the rain.

"What's the matter, John,...?" How many times have I told you that you get a fever when you get wet in the rain,...?" said mummy, rowing his head in the bath towel.

"I'm really sorry Mummy... I won't do it again."

And here too he brought out his old trick of escaping his mummy's quarrel.

"Okay,... It's okay,... Don't cry,..... "

Mummy's sweet words rang in his ears once more and he longed to hear the same mummy's words again.

"If my mummy had been there to scold me once more,...?"

He desperately wished, taking a deep breath and then walking back to his goal.

He was getting so close to the rest of the expectations he had been looking at so far, and John was still not willing to deliberately dismiss the belief that it might have been a road made of mud because those were the expectations he had held for so long.

He continued his journey through the jungle again. As he walked he would occasionally look into the valley, to see if any vehicles were going down the road below because he had seen muddy roads like this near his house and when he went trekking with Daddy he had often noticed large vehicles going by on such roads hoping that he might now be able to see any similar vehicle.

As he walked on, he saw another part of the valley very close,

"This road may also be a continuation of a distant road."

He was relieved to see the continuation of the same road so close to him that he did not have to walk very far anymore.

But as he got closer, he seemed to lose faith in the sights that appeared before him.

"Yeah, I know,.... this is an offroad and I've seen the same rocks and boulders on roads." He said many things and tried to comfort himself.

"Mummy is very scared to travel in big carriages that ply roads like this, but daddy and I are not at all afraid," he said to himself.

He was convinced that he could still see any such vehicle, but after a long time, it was getting dark in the air and he did not see a single vehicle passing by.

He was so frustrated that he bowed his head and then something on the ground caught his attention.

He took the object in his hands.

It was a piece of fishbone, not just one like this. Immediately a fountain burst forth from his eyes.

Is that spring enough to fill this dry river,...?

This is not a road, just a small river that has long since died.

But John was left there in the middle of a dead river with dead hopes, and soon darkness covered him.

It was a morning as the rays of the light slowly woke him up from his sleep and he was forced to get up even though he was a little upset.

The sound of the birds and the bright light of the sun combine to expose the beauty of the forest.

It was one of the most terrifying places he had ever been, but he was so amazed at how beautiful this place was now.

But the wonder on his face did not last long because the guilt about something in recent times has been following him mercilessly.

"Oops,... Why did I come here from that high place,...? It was enough to stay there without coming here anymore and if I were on the top of the mountain now I could see the views of the valley and the Views from the distance even if it was blurry so I could expect someone to help, but from here chances of getting help from others are very slim."

His aimless work through the vast jungle devastated him greatly, but he has no choice but to do so.

"Where am I going,....."

"Why should I go.....?"

"I am not going anywhere and I tried walking so much, only by giving me the juice that mummy used to make before me can I still have the energy to move on."

Having said this, he leaned against a nearby plant with a slight stubbornness.

"If I had been at home, I would have got everything I say right away, but now I don't get anything even though I wanted so much because mummy is no longer with me." He bowed his head with a swollen mind.

From that crowded woods somewhere he can hear a beautiful sound that rang in his ear.

"It can sometimes be the sound of water flowing."

Quickly John got up and walked in the direction of where he heard the sound and he was very curious about that expecting sight because, as daddy has said before, this kind of sound refers to the flow of water.

"The water usually flows from the highland to the lowlands, so I can reach the height by walking against the downstream water, can't I?"

He asked himself because the answer was made up in his own mind.

As he expected, it was a small stream, a beautiful stream flowing down from the heights between the small and large rocks and boulders.

"Wow,... Awesome,...." his lips whispered unknowingly to him.

The river was not obstructed by large branches of trees or small vegetation that stood between the rocks. Overcoming all the obstacles, overcoming depression in a frenzy without knowing what the end will be.

He took his eyes off the distant stream because what he had to pursue now was against the approaching stream, not with the flowing stream.

On either side of the stream, which looks like a rug, clinging to the mosses and wetting.

He began to advance upward, passing through the piles of rocks spread out like a carpet on either side of the stream.

After a short distance, he washed away the dirt that got stuck in his hand and clothes, but no matter how much he washes, it keeps repeating itself and which makes him very upset because he can never bear to have mud sticking to his clothes and bags his mummy bought him.

He looked back and realized that now he had come a long way but he was not ready to rest because his only first and last aim was to see the mummy somehow.

But as if to divert him from his aim,

the darkness that had established

power around him was an obstacle to his further journey and besides, the drops of water splashed on his face as he struggled to climb up on the rocks made him very uncomfortable.

He leaned back on the rock nearby determined to temporarily end his journey.

He had scratches and bruises on many parts of his legs and arms, but he had never felt this pain before.

It would sometimes be scratches and bruises when he slid off the rocks, and a small smile appeared on his face as he gently stroked his wounds as he saw his own wounds because Mummy would love him even more when he showed her the wounds.

His beautiful smile could be seen even in the darkness but it was still trying to cover John.

In the classroom, the kids are all so happy because as usual, it's their evening time so there is some time left to leave school.

But it's harder to wait for Mummy in these little times for John because he had so many questions filling his mind.

"Will mummy come now,...?"

"When will mummy come,...?"

"Will mummy be here by now,.....?"

About those hard situations, he had a long discussion with his mummy about such mental tensions. His mummy had taught him exactly how to face such a situation.

"There is nothing special to overcome, engage in activities that you enjoy, like drawing or reading and so on, ...In this way, you can reduce your thoughts about me when you are engrossed in activities of your choice".

The words that mummy had said while sitting in the car ran through his mind. He immediately pulled out a drawing book from his bag, held the pencil in his hand, and tried to draw, but there was no picture coming to his mind, only his mummy's face.

But by mistake, a picture of something accidentally got stuck in his mind.

Soon he wrote it down in the book, But there was also Mummy in it, along with baby John.

"How much more time is left to leave the school,...?"

"There's still a lot of time,..."

Said another boy, looking at the watch in his hand.

John was listening very carefully to this conversation between the children, in which another child's answer moistened his eyes and obstructed the drawing of his picture, and his tears fell on to his drawing and soon spread it around.

"Yes,... He's right, there's still some time left."

The variety of cars, trucks, and buses going along the road and so many different types of vehicles, big and small, kept watching to see if he could see his mummy's car somewhere in it.

He knows that what he is doing now is very futile because mummy will never come so soon.

Suddenly John heard someone talking to him about his mummy and looked out the door of the classroom,

"John,... your mummy has come, I saw your mummy waiting outside for you." After saying this, the boy disappeared.

When he heard his words he looked at the clock with a slight suspicion and saw that the clock's needle was pointing in the same direction as he had seen before.

"This is not the time for mummy to come regularly but mummy may have come earlier,..?"

He did not have time to wait for the answer to the question, and immediately he grabbed his bag and ran from the classroom.

While running, he had little doubt that the teacher would stop him from running because they say he would never go home once he fell into the hands of the teachers but luckily not a single teacher was on his way then.

After the stairs to the lower floor, he will reach the main gate of the school.

As he quickly descended the stairs a question flashed through his mind,

"Will the school warden open the gate for me,...?"

Of course, this was a very unexpected question for him,Soon his legs, which were running fast, suddenly stumbled and he fell down forcefully and very quickly without any expectation.

It was a terrible event, and his forehead hit the sharp edge of the stairs and he immediately felt like he was losing all control.

Attempts were made to prevent it from falling but the attempt was in vain.

He rolled down faster than he expected and was hit in many places, causing great injuries to his body, and in the end, he rolled down but could not get up from the impact of that fall.

Although he felt his vision begin to fade, he could still see some of the sights.

He realizes that someone is running up to him, picking him up and that someone has gathered around him, even though the view is still dim, and their voices.

"What happened John,....?"

"Are you still okay,...?"

"Don't worry,.... No problem at all,..."

But he could only silently shed tears in the face of their question.

"Take him to the hospital as soon as possible,..."

There were still many voices that could be heard by them but he could not react to anything and soon everything slowly became silent, even his gaze,...

CHAPTER SIX

"Everything is Okay,... You don't have to worry about it, it's because of a sudden shock,... I think you know about it. Although his accident was terrible, but

by the grace of God, he miraculously escaped...."

"John used to talk about mummy when he came to his senses, but I didn't call you because I didn't want you to be too sad at the time of his condition and he lost some blood in the fall, but he's now coming back to normal,... There's no point in you worrying like this."

He can hear someone talking around him, but all the time there is only darkness in his sight.

Slowly, passing through the veil of darkness, vague visions caught his eye,,.... It's quite vague.

He realized that there was someone around him and wanted to talk to them about something, but he couldn't move his body even the slightest, not even his tongue,...because he was so tired.

Conversations from around him again knocked on his ears,

" There was no point in you being so upset,... Come back,... Because you are lucky,... **Lilly,...."**

The call passed through his ears before he could descend again to the steps of his slumber.

"MUMMY,..."

Even though he was very tired, his surroundings underwent a very drastic change in his groan.

"Yes,... wonderful,... He opens his eyes, he is able to respond now,... Lilly, go back, we will manage it, sure."

"No,... mummy,... I'm okay, ... I want to see mummy right now, ..."

He does not even know where he had the power to say this because he was still very tired.

"Sweetie, ..."

It wasn't too long before Mummy's clear face was imprinted on his vague views, but Mummy was crying.

"What happened to you mummy,...?"

"Why is mummy crying,...?" My sweet mummy should never cry."

He did not notice a smile spread from his words on the faces of those around him but he did notice the smile on Mummy's face.

"Nothing baby,... I cried unknowingly..."

"Mummy, What's wrong with me,...?"

"How did I get here,...?"

"Are these all mummy's friends,...? "

"Nothing sweetie,... You just fell a little, that's all, there's nothing to be afraid of"

"It's okay mummy,... I have a secret to tell mummy"

John said to mummy with a little shyness, and by then the people around him had moved away, but John had never expected this.

Actually, he didn't pay attention to the others, he only cared about his mummy. John looked at those who were moving away in great amazement.

" What is that sweetie,......?"

Mummy came close to him to hear the secret, and he said to her again,

"It's not enough to get so close,

I can only tell you the secret if you come to me more."

He placed a kiss on the lips of his mummy, who was getting very close to him again.He whispered,

"I love you, mummy."

But all this was being noticed by those around him, and he felt ashamed of their affectionate smiles and immediately he hugged mummy.

But those affectionate moments did not last long. Blood began to ooze from his wound, and immediately the nurses and mummy who had been away ran to John to take care of him.

"John,... Are you okay,..?"

Mummy asked, gently tapping his head.

"No mummy,... I'm still in pain." With a small sigh, he responded to Mummy.

"Sister Lucy,... Administer 2.5ml Advil immediately to my son and it should be written in the clinical chart."

Mummy asked John, who was watching in amazement, a little angrily,

"How many times have I told you not to go down the stairs quickly,...."

"I'm sorry Mummy,... that was,..."

"You haven't been obeying my words lately," mummy continued in a little harder voice."

"Mummy, Are you mad at me,..?" He asked with horseradish eyes.

"No sweetie,... I said that unknowingly in my grief."

"That... Mu...mmy,... I,..,l was painting in class according to what mummy told me before. Then Jackson told me that Mummy had come, so I quickly stepped down the stairs to see mummy."

After a short pause, John thought of something and asked Mummy,

"I think mummy will be there even when I fall, but...Why didn't mummy save me? I thought mummy would save me even when I was falling."

"Oops, Oh my dear,... I wasn't there at the time, and it was your class teacher who called me and told me that you had fallen out of school in an accident and that's when I came to school,......You know how upset I was when they told me about you?"

"That is mummy,... I'm sorry,... I didn't know,... " he bowed his head in guilt.

"Okay,... It is okay dear,... "

"So, Was what Jackson told me a lie?"

"Maybe so,... " Mummy murmured.

"Mummy, did you see my wounds...? I'm in so much pain."

"It doesn't matter, Sweetie, they have given the medicine and you'll be well soon." Mummy stopped saying with a kiss.

"Mummy, you are so beautiful even when you are angry too,..."

John said to Mummy with words full of smiles, and he enjoyed the smile appearing on mummy's face too....

The water seeping through the boulders hit the stone and scattered into very small droplets and fell on his eyes, which made him very uneasy,...

He slowly opened his eyes from the clutches of sleep. But all of a sudden he was shocked to see that he was not lying in the same place where he was yesterday, but very close to the river.

If he had gone a little further, he would surely have fallen into the abyss.

His goals made him even more excited, and without wasting much time John collected water from the river and walked forward.

The distance he had traveled told him that he had come a long way.

Further heights are not far from him, Soon he has crossed the heights and the heights left him with spectacular views,

"Wow, ... Awesome,... Does this river originate from here,...?"

He had seen for the first time in his life the beautiful view of water gushing from the rocks, but he was not ready to go near it because when he was playing in the mud, mummy would tell him that there were dinosaurs and anaconda underground.

Mummy's words prompted him to reach his goal, and John stepped forward, overcoming that beautiful sight.

"Yes,... I think I have reached heights"

He approached the edge of the mountain, bounded by boulders, with trembling footsteps, and then there was a great Depth.

"The long abyss."

Even if there is little carelessness, and causing it to fall, the body will not be returned, and the body will be shattered and cut into pieces one by one. John seemed to have been warned there.

He was extremely frightened by this terrifying sight, but the desire to see his mummy made him a brave man.

Even in fear, he scrambled to the maximum end of the rock.

The strong wind passed by as if to push him away, but he did not fall because it was blowing against the abyss.

He can now see distant views, clouds spread out like a carpet at the heights, and forests that look like carpets below.

"Will there be a distance between highs and lows?"

"Don't the heights come from the lows? So,...Why is there so much distance between the forest and the sky? But far away, the forests are kissing the sky. Sure,.. "

He remained there, with all kinds of doubts and questions arising out of doubts.

If his mummy had been around, she would have answered all the questions. From a very young age, mummy would encourage him to ask every such question so she wouldn't ignore a single question of his.

Or if it was an unknown question for the mummy, mummy would say, "Find out the answer to this for my Sweetie yourself."

But now he has not yet got the answer to the question of where his mummy is, so the answer to that question is that he has come to find out for himself, he must have figured out the answer anyway it was a wish that touched his heart more than he wanted.

From the heights, he watched intently for the mummy but could not recognize anything like what had happened before. He was too scared to look to the bottom of the abyss, and could not even remember the terrible condition of the fall.

He could not understand anything in particular from the heights but did not want to go back because this was one of his last hopes and he had worked very hard to get here.

Unwilling to return, he left the edge of the cliff and went to safety. He could not take his eyes off the distance because his hopes were so far away from him, ...

His stomach was hungry, he tried to reach into the bag that had been set aside but could not reach out.

With a throbbing pain, he looked into the palm of hand, suffering minor bruises and scratches.

"Oh yeah,... Mummy has told me about this, God has given us such small stripes on our hands because there is a big secret behind it, if we want our hands to be folded, these lines are needed. Now it is because of these minor cuts and scratches that I am unable to clench my fists."

Earlier, he had noticed that his hand was cut off when he hit the sharp edges of the rock while climbing on the rocks on the river bank.

"I'm trying so hard to see mummy and yet I still can not do it,...?" With a small sigh, the question rising from the bottom of his mind drove his eyes slightly.

As he focused his gaze on the palm of his hand, he noticed three fingers, and behind all three fingers, there was a secret, the only secret he had carved out of his own,...(secret will be in next part).

Soon a beautiful smile appeared because of those three fingers, even in the midst of the blood drops and tears streaming down.

He opened his eyes with a little difficulty, and the strong wind that was still coming in front of him had brushed over him. He's very tired because he's struggled so hard to get to where he expected, yet the helplessness and guilt that his long-cherished hopes had suddenly gone in vain one day had left him exhausted.

However, his intense desire to see Mummy knocked him out of his sleep. He opened his eyes as hard as he could.

Once again he walked to the edge of the cliffs, perhaps because he had spent so much time here that he did not feel even the slightest hint of the fear he had felt before, and so quickly he had adapted to that hill slope. He stared into the distance.

"What is that,....?"

"Maybe that's a river, ... If it's a river, in the past when I went trucking with Daddy, most people used to stay by the river, and I still remember Daddy telling me earlier that everyone does it for the availability of drinking water. If that's the case, it means that there will surely be humans, and sometimes my mummy may be there too,...."

Even if these were words he had said once, he kept repeating the same thing.

He was very careful to see if he was seeing anything as he expected.

But.....

All of a sudden his legs slipped into the abyss, and he forgot about the imminent danger, eager to see if there was even a single chance left somewhere in the distance.

Within seconds he was down fast but his hand was caught in a small crack in the rock as if in indescribable luck.

He saw a large boulder falling to the depths before him until it disappeared, but there was no evidence that it had fallen to the abyss.

He had sustained serious injuries to both hands again, he realized that nothing more could be done with these hands.

It doesn't know why, neither mummy nor daddy came into his thoughts now, only fear, fear of death, and pain were still left.

He may be hanging for a long time and his hands are stretched out and he is in excruciating pain. He took his gaze from the depths and focused on his aching hands.

Here is another opportunity, one last chance. Perhaps it was his aching hands that became the motivation for his escape.

No matter how much he moved, he would never fall, "he realized very quickly that he was not holding the rock, the rock was holding him.

That realization and the intense pain soon turned him into a real warrior.

"Yes,... The real warrior for his life."

His start was from excruciating pain, and he tried to rise to the top, enduring excruciating pain, never ready to give up. He immediately positioned himself on top of the rock with his other hand and pressed his legs firmly against the rock.

Now he can control his weight. Tried to pull the trapped hand, but could not. The realization that he could escape from there forever only with the help of his trapped hand made him continue his quest again because his mind murmured to him that,

"Nothing is going to be possible without being able to do it, it must be done no matter what."

Each time he tried, his hands kept getting sore again and again, but it did not hurt him at all.

At last, at the end of his long effort, his hand came out of the bow of that rock, and now everything is so much easier because he has become a real warrior.

John escaped from the abyss of death, not wanting to stay there any longer, and ran away, aiming as he came, Forever,...

without looking back, ...

CHAPTER SEVEN

What Daddy had told him before this survival in the forest was so valuable that he was relieved by the survival strategies that Daddy had told him when he was having trouble in this forest, and he would have remembered it.

One of them was to put a mark all along the way so that he could be prevented from getting out of the way and getting caught in danger, but there was still a sense of guilt left in his mind because if he had used the same trick before, he wouldn't have lost his big bag.

Then second, Daddy would use the compass, and John understood how to walk with any sign on the way he walked, but he didn't know how to use the compass because when John held it in his hands, the needle would keep spinning, but it wouldn't move from Daddy's hand.

Suddenly he was frightened by the sight in front of him, but because of its strong smell, he had unknowingly covered his nose.

It was the decaying carcass of an animal, and he could see the bones and teeth of that creature, and he was disgusted by the creeping worms and insects.

Although the sights in front of him were disgusting to him, he walked towards the corpse, curious to know some things.

Some of the insects on top of it tried to catch it on his hands and face but he snatched it away in disgust.

The smell was beyond endurance as he walked so he noticed that he was holding his nose tightly, but he did not feel shortness of breath because he was breathing that dirty air through his mouth very excitedly but he could not understand this fact at the time because he did not feel the foul odor that he feels when he breathes through his mouth as like when he breathes from the nose.

He couldn't understand anything in particular when he saw the rotten body and bones, but its pointed teeth caught his attention.

"Pointed-edged teeth"

Perhaps it was a carnivore because Daddy had said that only carnivorous creatures would have pointed claws and teeth. John shook his head as if he understood something.

"How could this creature have died here?"

He took turns trying to find out, but despite his best efforts, he couldn't figure out how it died.

However, he did not disappoint but continued to try, but his effort was in vain.

Perhaps it was because he had inhaled that dirty breath for so long that he began to feel uneasy.

He immediately tried to get away from there.

But it was then that he realized from himself a brutal truth hidden by this forest, not only that he didn't remember the way he had come, but he was surrounded by bushes larger than him, so he couldn't see distant sights.

The bushes had detained him so that he couldn't move a bit.

He decided to walk back the way he came last but no matter how hard he tried he could not even remember the way he came.

He realized that he was in real danger, that he was getting more and more in danger as he tried to get out, and while searching for a way out, he stumbled upon a plant but did not get any injuries, but his shoe got stuck between its roots.

He can never leave that shoe there because it is the memory of his mummy so he took it out with great difficulty and at the same time his attention was suddenly focused on that root again. He can understand some things now,

"I think sometimes it's the root of a tree, so somehow I can climb up the tree and figure out the way out."

Immediately he searched all around for a tree but he could not find even a small tree anywhere in the bushes.

He tries to climb to the top of a plant, which is only a bush, but it falls to the ground because it cannot bear his weight.

But still, he only makes himself more vulnerable, because he does not even remember the place where he had been until now, but from somewhere the stench of the corpse returned to his nose, and he decided to go back there because he did not know any other way. After all, that stink was the only guide in the bush.

So after a while, he reached the rest of the body in the forest.That's when he came up with an idea,

"It's only because of this stench that I'm able to come back here exactly now. Likewise, if I have any memory of any smell outside these bushes and follow it, I can reach the end of these bushes."

But this is an idea he could never have imagined because a long time ago he was coming through these bushes.

It was not too long before he could now understand the answer to a question he had not previously received, that is, this would be the same beast that had strayed into the bushes like him before him.

This animal may have tried hard to get out but could not, So it may have died without food here because this creature with sharp claws and teeth can never quench its hunger by eating plants.

"Poor beast, this beast should have been still alive. Why did God kill this creature before I came,...? If this beast had been with me, we could have escaped from this jungle together because our only goal is to escape from this bush, That's it.." John comforted his eyes.

Suddenly a thought passed through his mind and he immediately opened the bag that was nearby and he was very relieved to see the chocolates and water inside because he had stored a lot of chocolates and water in the small bag before leaving the big bag.

"Anyway, I don't have any problem, I do not have to starve to death like this creature." He ate very little chocolate from inside the little bag.

John is playing a phone game in his room, and while playing, mummy's voice taps on his ears,

"John,... John,..... Come here and take your dinner "

But he didn't respond to mummy's words because he's the most loved game he's playing now. But there was no sign of his mummy's call stopping, and again, her loud voice disturbed him very much, but he didn't answer, and John was still engrossed in his games.

As soon as he finally heard the door of his room open violently, John hid the phone under the pillow and covered his head with a blanket, and pretended to be sleeping.

"Sweetie,... Sweetie,.. Wake up, your dinner is ready...."

"Oops,... Yes mummy,... I'm coming...."

Mummy picked him up and walked downstairs.

"Sweetie,.. Were you sleeping,..? " mummy asked.

"Yes mummy I was,.. " John nodded his head.

"Lately you've been sleeping before dinner, you'll get sick if you do not eat dinner that's why I woke you up," mummy said.

"It's okay mummy,.. I love you...."

He answered mummy very affectionately but he was very angry with mummy for harassing him while playing but he did not show it out.

Mummy again continued,

"John,.. Do you know how many times I have called you,...?"

But John did not answer Mummy's question, and he pretended not to hear. Sure he knew Mummy would have noticed it but he didn't say anything because his mind was full of the sadness of losing the game.

Mummy came to the dinner table and put him in a chair that was there and then put his favorite food in front of him.

'It was soup.'

He's always loved the smell of mummy's soup, but he's not ready to eat.

" Sweetie,... Do you know what I've made for you,...? Your favorite chicken soup." Mummy said, patting his soft cheek.

But John lifted his hands and knocked his mummy's hand away angrily,

"I don't like you and your food too,... "

He looked at the mummy's face very angrily and said, but he never intended to say this, but it came out of his mouth without knowing it.

John immediately got up from his chair and went up the stairs to his room. While walking away he looked at his mummy's face again, he saw that his mummy was standing there and looking at him with a lot of sadness and tears in her eyes.

Seeing this sight, his eyes were filled with tears and his heart was broken.

Mummy may never expect John to do this, and that was probably why she was so upset that he could understand it with a sense of guilt.

John too wanted to hug his mummy and apologize, but in the intensity of his anger, he rejected them all that sad face of his mummy was so heartbreaking that he could never forget it.

"Mummy,... "

There's only darkness all around... And a very ugly stench... He began to understand almost everything about what was going on in him.

He can see mummy's face even if it's only dark all around him, Mummy's face in memories, Yes,... That the same face of mummy who was hurt in his word,... and it doesn't fade from his mind no matter how hard he tries.

"Mummy,... I'm so sorry... I really love you,.... "

Unbeknownst to him, a little groan rose in him, but even in that little groan, the surroundings had undergone a very big change. The many strange sounds, moving past the silence, are disturbed as if the surrounding plants were afraid of something. It didn't take him long to realize that these were signs of some danger that he didn't know about around him, but he wasn't afraid of any of this because there was only guilt in his mind.

"Mummy,... I'm so sorry and I really love you,.... "

His loud voice, which penetrated the fear of the dark, could sometimes be heard even beyond the bushes.

CHAPTER EIGHT

He opened his eyes.

It was a beautiful morning but only the strangeness around him, even though he had unconsciously enjoyed the beauty of the forest.

The body of the animal in front of him is almost entirely still dissolved in the ground, only the bones remain, but its stench has not made him as unbearable now as before because he had almost come to terms with his surroundings.

" I wanted to get out somehow, I'll never be able to see mummy if I just sit here."

" Maybe my mummy is looking for me in this big forest like this,...? Has my mummy gone looking for me all over the place,....?"

Disturbed by so many thoughts, John raised his head to the bushes taller than he was and asked.

"How can I get out of here,...? Can I,......?"

"If I'd been taller than Daddy, I'd be able to figure out a way to get out. But I can't do it now because I'm still daddy's and mummy's baby."

After a short silence, he again continued,

"I can only get out of here if I've grown taller than Daddy,but by then the rest of the food will be gone....?" His eyes fell again on the bones of the remaining animal.

"Am I going to die,...? No, I'm only going to die once I see my mummy one last time.I have to get out somehow, no matter how hard it is"

He searched around with tears in his eyes, but no idea came to his mind.

He was most troubled by the realization that plants taller than him were plants that couldn't bear his weight, even if they were around him.

He lifted his eyes to the sky, the clouds moving away in a panic, not knowing where to go,...

Soon he realized that the white sky was also being covered with darkness.

" The heavens and the earth are everything,... How beautiful is everything,..."

"Could all this be God's creation?"

"God..... Does God still live? Where is God,....?"

"If God had existed, wouldn't he have saved me from here,...?"

"No,... I should never doubt God because God is great and, ... God, I love you so much even though you are not saving me from here because you gave me a good daddy and mummy,.... and ever you are my Almighty God,... Ever,... Amen."

John opened his eyes and looked around and realized that unexpected events had left him with his little prayer, the bushes are slanting as if they were about to fall to the ground by a strong wind that doesn't even know where it is from, and his mind goes through so many thoughts that he can't control them.

The memories that break him are now in his favor, and the lost courage and confidence are now replete with him.

Seeing birds flying in the sky, his mind speaks to him, from the light of memories.

"Where are these birds going,....?"

"They try to get back into their cage before the sky gets dark,... These are the same birds I've seen in the woods before, and their nest sits on top of that big tree. And,... Then if I follow these birds, I can escape from here forever because they fly so high that they can see the other side of these big bushes"

Then he was not prepared to waste much time, and he rushed forward, following the birds flying in the sky under the bushy forest, but while running something suddenly came back as if he had suddenly remembered something and continued to run forward after picking up his bag.

Although the birds flying in front of him occasionally disappeared from his sight, they were very helpful to him because they were birds flying in groups and their speed was also interrupted by the strong wind.

Looking back, he had traveled a long way, but had not yet been able to reach the other side of the forest.

'Doubts tried to dissuade him but expectations persuaded him to move on."

It was not too long before tall trees had appeared slightly before his eyes through those large bushes, but by then the birds that had guided him had overtaken him and disappeared. Immediately he came to the other side of the bush.

He looked away from the top of the great boulder that was there, and now those bushes were lower than he was, and he saw the borderless bushes stretching farther and wider, but were still grounded by the strong wind that passed them by.

CHAPTER NINE

On the way, he saw a big fallen tree and the tree seems to have fallen for a long time because all of the inner stems except the bark have almost decayed in the rain and sunlight and there are cracks in the outer bark but the bark is thick.

John saw the fallen tree and had an idea for something and soon he walked near to that fallen tree and tried to climb on the top of it.

It is a bit big, but somehow he struggled to climb on top of it, balanced, and slowly practiced standing and walking on the tree.

From time to time he would jump hard on the tree but it would not shatter except to shake slightly. After standing still for a while, he stood on the top of the tree and looked around the forest in amazement.

"By now I must have grown up more than my mummy"

John said looking down but suddenly he remember again what he had just said earlier, "mummy"

"Yes, I want to see mummy,....Okay, enough,... come on,..I am going to see my mummy,...."

He tried to jump from the top to the bottom but a fear of something did not allow him and In the end, with his continued try he realized one thing great fear that he could not go down and he did not have the courage even to look down so John decided to do it because he could not find any ways to get down soon he sat down and tried to jump down again by closing his eyes but still he could not.

"It was enough to have mummy somewhere, mummy will let me down if I cry once,... but...Who will come and help me now,....?"

He looked around helplessly for help and he came to know that there is no one around him except the useless trees and plants because that was silent before his question and his needs.

The atmosphere became very quiet as if those must have seen this horrible condition of his.

Unbeknownst to him, tears flowed down from his eyes and he assured that no one was going to see his cries and tears even his mummy.

He was not ready to give up even though the situation was so unfavorable.

" If I fall, let me fall,... I don't have any problems, maybe after the fall, there will be injuries and pain and nothing more is going to happen because of how much I have endured all this in my life."

John tried to get down by pulling on the small branches that were in the tree itself and he stretched out his short leg and tried to touch the ground but could not because this fallen tree is so much bigger than him.

But his current situation that's much more difficult than before. because he understood that he was really stuck because he could not go back up and down.

Unable to do anything, he clung to the tree with his shivering hands.

He raised his head in fear and looked at the small horn he was holding, it was so dry.

He could only stare at it and could do nothing. yet released from a narrow distinctive sound that the horn could not bear all his weight.

The horn was about to break, that realization made him cry a lot, and soon called out to his mummy loudly for help but he could understand it was never going to happen.

However, his frightened cries did not last long in the forest and suddenly his cries stopped with a small sound.

He let go of the grip of fear, and opened his eyes and he was sure he had fallen but he did not feel any pain because the whole place where he had fallen was covered with the decaying leaves of the same tree.

By this, he felt as if he had fallen into a very smooth bed.

The broken horn Is still in his hand and he looked at that broken horn with a smile.

"Jumping was enough and there was nothing to fear"

John realized that the height he had seen from above was not the same as when he looked down but he was not too happy about anything anymore.

" How happy would I be if I saw my mummy like this?"

He got up from there and ran closer to the fallen tree and said giving a kiss,

" I love you,..... you scare me a little but don't worry I am still in love with you,....."

After saying goodbye to that fallen tree he walked away and soon the forest covered him.

The variety of birds, flowers, and plants passed by John and he noticed butterflies circling in front of him and he be can to tell each color,

"Blue,... violet,...and yellow,..."

As he walked forward, he recognized a rising voice that stunned the silence of the forest, he soon followed that sound and ran in the direction where the sound was coming from.

John remembered everything daddy had said before while running because he would often hear that sound when he went trucking with daddy.

When daddy hears this sound, he says that water is flowing somewhere nearby.

He was so happy to see the water flowing all that time that the same joy still excites him now and follows the beautiful sound of that river and the anxiety of wanting to see something is reflected on his face. Soon he realized that the voice came very close to him.

At last, he began to see the river a little through the overgrown vegetation and the warmth of that river sucked him slowly and an expected tremor passed through his body.

Unexpectedly, his legs sank somewhere and he tried to escape by grabbing hold of the branch of a nearby plant because his legs were stuck in a muddy pit and the shoes that mummy brought for him also sank into the mud.

His eyes were full because his shoes were all mud and it was a shoe that mummy had so lovingly brought before she went to see daddy.

Mummy had already told him not to get dirty, but.....

Unfortunately, the branch of the plant was already broken but he tried to climb out of the pit before the broken branches were completely broken.

Eventually, with great difficulty, he climbed out of the pit before breaking. All the joys that had been there for so long are now lost.

"It was a white shoe that mummy bought and now it is brown and if mummy sees it, she will scold me"

He was not ready to stop crying and wiped away the tears flowing with his hand.

John looked at his hand as he felt something uncomfortable when he wiped away the tears, something that looked like it belonged to the plant was clinging to both his hands.

Perhaps, it was the stain of that plant, he understood.

But he had already wiped his eyes and had a trace of the stain on his eyes, soon he ran near to the water with teary eyes.

Mummy has said earlier that if something goes wrong in your eyes, do not scratch it and just rinse it off with water.

He was not able to open his eyes fully because of the burning eyes so he fell in many places and injured many parts of his body but he ran forward with the bruises and finally he reached the river and washed his eyes in the water and continued until the pain in his eyes subsided.

The pain subsided, he slowly opened his eyes after his prolonged pain and was amazed to see the amazing sights around him. What the river hid before him were some very wonderful experiences and memories.

Daddy's words talking about the river echoed as if daddy was next to him and now he can see in his blurred eyes his beloved dad standing next to him.

Daddy was talking to him about something,... but he couldn't hear anything that daddy is saying,

However, he nodded his head as he heard but the cold breeze that blew across the river made him refuse to do so.

Every moment that mummy held him close and kissed him passed through his memories.

Unbeknownst to him, he whispered in his mind "Mummy"

Shortly at that moment of time something struck him in mind,

"Where is my Mickey,....?"

He searched for Mickey in his arms and bag but could not find it.

He wanted it more because he loved it more even though it had no particular reasons.

John remembered a few things that he had left Mickey downstairs, who had previously been in his hand to take chocolates out of his bag and forget to pick up the Mickey again.

This memory also made him very tired and he looked at the empty hand with a depressed mind and wished it was enough to have Mickey.

He sat on the rock near the river and cried for Mickey,

"Mickey,...I miss you,... I missed you because of me and my mistake,...I should never have missed you,... but I lost you now,..."

While crying, he turned his attention to the shoes that mummy had brought.

The shoes were covered with mud all over and he immediately took off his shoes and washed them in running water but no matter how much he washed, he could not recover the same color that the mummy had bought.

Realizing that nothing could be done with him, John himself give up the effort but by then he was started to step back into his old memories.

Mummy bought him these shoes at that the day before he was going to see daddy.

There were so many shoes in black, brown, red and white and so much more,.... but his favorite was the white shoe and his mummy liked it too.

When the shop lady wrapped the shoe and handed it to him, he gave it to the mummy and also promised that,

"I will keep these shoes from getting dirty "

What a wonderful days that all was and those were unforgettable days for him and he knew very well that it didn't matter how much he was worried anymore.

"Wait until mummy comes back once and mummy comes, I will cry and tell her that my shoes are solid first,...I just have to cry in front of my mummy and she will just say, "Don't worry,.. it is all okay" and she will hug me with love because I am her little baby boy" John said with a smile.

He asked his doubt as he looked at the flowing water,

" Who said if you look at the water, you will see your face?"But I cannot see my face right now,... I learned in school that if you look at the water, you will see your face but I know it is everything wrong that's why children fall asleep in classes."

"But if I fall asleep unknowingly in any class, the teachers will tell my mummy and scold too,.. "

John also saw some fish approaching him in the river looking for John who was standing aside.

Occasionally some fish come up out of the water and look at him and then sink to the bottom and some fish jump over the water making a small noise as if they were happy.

"Are these fish practicing high jump to compete,....? "I used to practice high jump in my school too "

He noticed a group of small fish approaching as if to speak,

" Oh,... sometime they may not know me because I am coming to this forest for the first time"

Even if he moves a little, they are scared,

"Hello,... my name is John and let me be your friend?"

He continued, even though he knew there would be no response from their side to his question.

"And,... I am very upset now because

I lost my mummy,...Have you seen my mummy,...?"

But he didn't get any answer to his question which made him a little nervous.

"Can you tell me please,...?"

John again asked because he very much wanted to see his mummy.

Even though he knows that question will never be answered, he keeps asking because of the desire in his heart.

He looked around and he could only hear the silent trees and the sound of the wind and also the sound of light breeze but none of this is the answer to his question.

But by then he was fascinated by the beauty of the river, trees, and plants that stood as if they were about to fall into the river, and the vines that touched the water like kissing the river.

The river that tries to run away somewhere in a trance without knowing what the end is, and the breeze that blows over John hugs him affectionately.

Absolutely John is very free now, but even in the midst of this freedom, the thought that Mummy is nowhere near is breaking him down.

For a while, the river was erasing his troubles and faint memories without him knowing it.

In the meanwhile, he saw crabs hiding among the stones, which at first frightened him a little, but the fear disappeared with the cool breeze.

Though he was fascinated by the river, he was not ready to venture into the water because he was very afraid,... Besides, if mummy comes now, surely mummy will argue with him.

All he did was enjoy the beauty of the river from the riverbank, but in the distance, John realized that the river was trying to hide something from him because there was something big white in the distance that caught his eyes.

"Yes,... I can see that in the distance but not from this forest anyway..." He made up his mind.

"What could that be,....?"

Doubt filled his inside and soon desire too...

He had to cross this river to see it but when he saw the river he was very scared and gave up his attempt there... But the desire for that filled his heart and compelled him to do so but he could not.

" Will I fall into this water,...?"

"Will I die...?"

"Will the snake bite me from inside the water,...?" because mummy has told me before, that they all live in water"

"What do I do if a shark attacks me from under the water,....?"

Many unanswered questions arose in his mind and soon he left his doubt and returned to the forest.

The next day,... It was also a good morning and this day was also ready to pass like a normal day, the desire to see his mummy woke him up from his sleep.

He again reached the river bank to collect water from the river before leaving, soon the desire approached him this time as usual.

"I need to know what that is,...?"

He decided to cross the river and made sure that he did not have as much fear as before.

John put his feet into the following cold water but it was not only now that he realized the mistake was not as bad as he thought it would be because the river was shallow.

But he still had a small fear in his mind that he would fall because of the force of the following water, however, he was not ready to go back because he had crossed almost half of the river.

As he walked, John somehow managed to get to the other side, moving away from the deeper area and climbing over the rocks because his dad has clearly taught him how to deal with situations like this.

Although fear occasionally shook his legs, he knew from his experiences that there was no point in being a fear.

"Yes I won,..."

He said, looking back at the Misfortunes he had overcome, the rest is very easy to cross and only a small flow is left so John felt a little relieved.

He looks at the object in the distance are now it is almost close to him, and the curiosity arose in him as to what it would be.

Unexpectedly, his legs slipped due to the lubrication and he was about to fall hard, he had tried to prevent him from falling with his hand but the fall was so strong that the hand and the head strongly swung over the rock that was there.

For a moment his consciousness was gone, and he felt nothing but a frenzy, but he tried to get up with the help of something. He got up and opened his eyes and closed his eyes on the situation that he doesn't see anything.

As darkness fell on his eyes, he could not do anything even to cry because he was dizzy.

Unfortunately, the legs slipped again and fell backward, luckily there was a puddle behind him and he could feel the mud dripping down his face, understood the things around him but was unable to imperil finer so his attempt to get up failed.

Slowly the darkness tries to cover his eyes as he looks up at the sky, the body tries to become stationed and the mind whispers, as in his eagerness to know something,.......

" Am I going to die,...?"

"Is this the experience that I have when dying,....?" It is better to die than not to see my mummy,..... But,... if only I could see mummy for the last time,"

"I want to see mummy"

His mind whispered from the depth of the drowsiness, opened his eyes as if his soul joined back on him himself, yet the body remained motionless as before.

He lay there for some time without being able to get up.

"Was I going down into the mud,...?"

Because he noticed that muddy water was rising up to his mouth and nose.

All of a sudden his detached old strength in the body was regained, and even if he had stood.

He was weary and the force to stand had not been left in him and he was reclining on the big rock that was on the edge with what could not get up.

A small drop of blood crossed his eyes and fell on his after being illuminated by the sun on the opposite side,...... Like a shining red diamond.

John became suspicious of the sight and rubbed his hand against his head and saw nothing clearly because his vision was blurred, but he realized that he had suffered a serious head injury when he saw bloodstains on his hand.

"Should I cry,......?"

"Should I not cry,......?"

"Do I have any advantages in crying,...?" Despite the unbearable pain, his mind asked him.

"No,.. Never,... I will never cry,..."

He said in a stumbled voice but before that the tears were separated from his eyes.

He saw someone walking towards him from a distance that he had seen that man somewhere but he clearly didn't know about the person despite how many searched in his memories.

A little closer, John understood that there are wounds all over his body. The stranger spoke to him,

"Isn't your mummy a doctor,...? Can you tell mummy about my wounds,...? I think your mummy will help me if you say."

"For that, I don't even know where my mummy is," John answered.

"But I know,... your mummy is there"

The stranger said, pointing to that crushed flight. John saw the mummy standing in the same spot as the stranger pointed out, and soon John ran to the mummy.

While running, John called out,

"Mummy,... Why don't you help them,..?"

"No, I will never help them because they are the ones who separated you and me forever,..." Mummy answered.

"But mummy,... isn't it because of them that I just found my mummy right now?"

Now mummy did not answer his question and he did not get mummy's answer but tried to run towards mummy but mummy was so far away than he expected.

Soon his body and mind came together. All he saw were fantasies that had unknowingly evoked, he looked away and saw no one there,...

"How many dreams will I have seen about mummy after mummy parted,..... Too much.But I do not know when I saw any of the dreams I had because my mind says I've just seen all the dreams and that's what drives me to see mummy,..."

"Dreams never exist, but...... Dreams arise from Memories so, Memories Never going to exist .If so, Don't Desire to arise from Memories and Dreams,....? So, will the Desire exist,....?"

"Let us go see mummy anyway,..."

John stood up and noticed that mud was sticking to his body and went down to the river and almost washed it off with water but he could not wash it off completely.

In such a short time he had learned some things about the river, he understood that this river with its beautiful face had hidden another face of cruelty, but that did not deter him, because he believed that there was a cruel face behind everything except his own mummy's face.

He continued to his destination and soon he realized that it was the wreckage of a plane just as he Imagined.

" It was the last plane I boarded", he murmured.

He had already recognized some of the last letters he had read before boarding the flight and saw some of the seats of the same flight scattered around.

"My mummy and I sat in similar seats like this,..." he covered his eyes with his hand.

There's something around him trying to hunt him. But they are not just wild beasts, they are just memories..... sharp memories that belong only to him.

"The last moment I had with my mummy." Those were the moments he could never forget and desperately wanted to go back to those same memories.

There was a very unbearable pungent smell in the surroundings, and John pressed his nose very hard because he could not bear it. He often feels as if he's going to be dizzy because of the harsh smell that exists in the air. But he still couldn't understand why this smell was so strong because It was all the first experience of his life.

"Where does such an unbearable smell come from?"

He had almost forgotten about the danger of the jungle in his eagerness to find out what it was hiding soon after.

He tried to aim his way through the overgrown bushes in the sense that it would surely swallow him up, but an unexpected sight blocked his eyes, a little farther along the river,... Even though he could see it from a distance, nothing could be confirmed but doubts lingered in him even if he understood it because that view is one of the things he is most familiar with.

He approached there with hope. Surely it must have been a man-made one so of course, human habitation took place here, His mind began to tell him.

As he got closer he realized that it was a tent .... But none of the tents he had seen before were like this, but it was made of cloth and various parts of the airplane and they must have worked very hard to make it anyway.

The expectation that there would definitely be humans there comforted his mind a lot, but despite searching for a long time he could not find anyone around there but still he had not entered the tent due to some minor disturbance.

Yet he decided to enter, perhaps even if someone was sleeping inside it?

He saw a view closer to the entrance and quickly ran back.

A cobweb was woven right in front of him, and if he had stepped a little further without noticing it would have landed on his face.

John was frightened not only by the sight of the spider web in front of him but also by the fact that there was a big spider inside that he had never seen before in his life.

John was so afraid of spiders that his mummy would tell him that spiders were dangerous and that its venom made it even more dangerous.

However, he did not want to back down. He took a small stick from the ground, removed it from in front of him, opened the tent, and went inside.

By then he was frightened by the sight inside, not one or two but many spiders and spider webs but there was no need to be afraid of it now, they would only attack us if we attacked them and he went inside without too much fear.

But what hid him inside the tent was a sight that hide many secrets, and the evidence that someone had lived here widened his eyes.

In the meantime, he noticed a book that had just been opened and it was an unfinished book written by someone because the last page of the book was marked with a pen.

Even though John did not need it, the pages of that book searched for something.

He noticed that the word "survival" was more pronounced in it, but he was still very upset by the pungent odor that permeated his nose.

The book in his hand was folded up and placed there safely and he was busy discovering new things that were still hidden around him.

The seats of the fallen flight, the wood piled up on one side, the burning marks, and so on.

A glimpse of something in between had fascinated him so much that in so many packets a variety of fruits had been stored, and chocolates and breads had kept everything that was necessary to survive in this big forest.

He also saw the cake that was left open to him, and soon he took a small part of it and put it in his mouth, but it didn't taste as good as he thought. He spits it out because that cake is not edible and it was soaked and tasted ugly.

Yet he never gave up thinking that the food wrapped in the packets might have been spoiled like this because now he really understands why his mummy often argues with him when he opens the food while he is at home.

He often noticed that Mummy always kept food wrapped and stored, and had previously told him that the purpose of storing food in packets like this was to keep it for a long time without spoiling it.

But John did not take any food from there for him because it was all someone else's and Mummy would always forbid him from taking other people's belongings without their consent.

As he was about to turn around anxiously, a small creature saw John and seemed to be frightened and quickly disappeared across him.

John, too, was afraid of a sudden incident because it was an unexpected thing. He noticed something falling out of the hand of the little creature running away at high speed, and he walked up to it, 'It was a piece of bread.'

Now that he really saw the surroundings more clearly than before, everything was so cluttered that only the dust, the speckles, and the spider webs were left in this tent.

That means, there's no human habitation here, and everyone may have migrated from here sometimes.

"Sure, there was no human habitation left here. If they had stayed, they would never have lived in such a filthy place."

As he was about to leave, John turned around and walked over to the food, where he noticed a large packet nearby. It was the cover of some shop, in which he read the shop's name and address, and then he began to store inside it one by one the food items he liked, and he didn't have any particular doubts, since most of those food items had been bought by mummy before.

By then, the packet was too heavy.

It could not be carried away by him so he left some of it and collected some others in the small bag and John went ahead adjusting the weight of the big packet.

As soon as he remembered something he left and stuffed the food back into the big packet because this was all he needed to live in this vast forest so he began to realize the importance of food.

But the weight of it was still too much for him to bear.

It was then that he accidentally saw a skateboard wrapped and stored next to him, and there was a letter on the back of it,

"To dear Jerry"

John pulled out the note with great sadness.

"Yes...... This is an accident that has ended everyone's expectations, even of my mummy,..."

And then it was all very easy for him.

At the end of his long efforts, he was able to carry everything near to the river bank but, he again realized the great difficulty that was still left before him.

"How do I get it across the river?"

He didn't seem to have any particular way to do that.

It is the flowing river, which is more likely to fall by the force of the flow because he had already believed that he could never trust this river anymore.

So he packed his little bag as much as possible and decided to cross over to the other side of the river, and did the same.

As a result of the fact that he continued this many times, he was able to deliver all the food safely to the other side of the river, and then it was filled back in the same packet, and everything was stored close to the fallen tree and placed securely.

He looked up again at the rest of the plane's ruins from the riverbank,

"Yes,... It's quite trying to hide secrets. I must know those hidden secrets," he said,"

His mind was full of eagerness to know them all, so there was no mind with a mind to leave.

A very foul order came unexpectedly and penetrated through his nose.

The question remained in his mind as to where this foul smell was coming from?

But he did not pay attention to it because all his attention and thoughts were on his old memories.

Not long after, he saw a dead body lying too close to him, paralyzing his vision.

At first, he realized one thing, this dead body belonged to a man, and it was the shirts and pants of the corpse that helped him do it.

He approached the dead body with stumbling legs and teary eyes.

Even if what he sees is a corpse of a man, it seems to John in a very strange way that someone has put mud on top of it, half of it covered with mud.

"Whose dead body is this,....?"

"Who covered this dead body with soil,...?"

" Aren't they human,....? Aren't they burying dead bodies in the ground,....? Because mummy has told me about it,...So are there still humans in this vast forest?"

He loudly begged someone for help,

"Hello.... is anyone here,...? Can you hear me, Mummy,...? Are you here,...?"

But he did not get the answers he was hoping for.

As his voice rose, many strange noises rose from the forest, the birds soar into the sky as if frightened by something.

Suddenly, there was an unexpected change in the forest that was quiet,

"Or would not the Corpus be completely buried in the ground even if they were humans,...?"

Overcoming that odor that disturbed his nose, he walked closer to the Corpse. He tried to talk to the dead body, even though he already knew it was dead.

"Hello uncle,.... Can you hear me,....?"

He didn't get any answer as he expected, however he wanted to know who's dead body was.

John couldn't recognize the face because the head of the body was immersed in the soil.

He grabbed its hair and pulled it out.

At the end of the effort, the whole head came out of the soil but when John saw its face, he trembled with fear because its face was completely dissolved in dust and the eyes protruding with the teeth were clearly visible.

Most of the bones of the face can be visible and the head is covered with worms that eat the carcass.

Anyway it was a horrible face,... though he was afraid at the sight of that terrifying face he concealed his fear.

However, he was very curious to know whose body it was.

Suddenly he realized something and walked closer to the corpus again,

and removed the soil from the side of the corpse's pocket, and pulled something out of its pocket.

He was convinced that he could identify this person from what he had just received.

"ADAM JAMES LARRY"

He worked very hard to read the name on that card because the letters were beginning to fade. The face of the person seen on that card made some changes in his expressions.

"I have seen this person somewhere,.?"

"Is this that Businessman,...? Yes,... I still remember. He was the only one who got angry with the air hostess on that day,...."

He was proud of himself for being able to invent something by himself.

"Yes,... I have discovered. As daddy said, I can be a detective officer," John said proudly to himself.

But John understood with great sadness that not only a body like this but some more remain. He visited each of the bodies and collected evidence, but did not receive from some and as he understood them from those who received.

He has seen every person who recognized at least once before. But he did not feel tired, even though it was a terrifying look.

He continued in his important work. Everything was covered with mud like an old corpse.

He removed the soil and collected the evidence he needed, like a detective officer.

As he visited each corpse a question would break into his mind," Would this be my mummy? "

Because like everyone else, he had never seen his mummy since the accident.

So John now had his strong desire that no corpses he saw should be his mummy because he should not look like his mummy as dead, should look like his own living mummy,......

But he saw a dead body so unexpectedly and he felt like he had lost all hope because all he had seen so far were the corpses of men but now in front of him was a woman....

When he saw that particular body, he was tired of going there because many thoughts about mummy arose in him.

One thing is for sure though, it is not his mummy because he does not really remember the clothes mummy is wearing but this is not the mummy's hair color but doubt haunts him.

The head of the body was also immersed in the soil and John grabbed it by the hair.

He was very frightened to see its eyes staring at him, which had parted from the corpse but he could not recognize the dead body because there was nothing left in the body to identify it.

He gave up the attempt because he was sure it was not mummy.

John walked back, this was the only body found in the distance about him and he stored the identity cards he had collected and put those in his bag.

"One, two, three, four,... so far I have found five dead bodies but I did not get the identity card of the fifth aunty and I got the remaining four uncles." He said to himself.

John knows all four of them well but he only didn't know about aunty, he did not want to know more about that aunty because it is not his mummy anyway.

The purse, identity card, and watch collected from the corpses were kept in his bag so that nothing could be lost because all these are very precious things before him and he felt a little proud of his intelligent move.

"As my daddy said, I'm an intelligent detective officer", he made up his mind.

He walked again to the same part where the parts of the crashed plane were left, but now his mind was hurting him because he had walked so close to the same plane before but that was the moment when he was very happy with his mummy.

Suddenly, his attention shifted to one side and a photo fell to the ground,

That was a family photo.

He picked up the photo and looked at each of the people in it.

"A daddy,... mummy,.... and two small children,..."

He knows the Mummy in the photo very well because he has seen her before, it was when he saw the two children in it that John remembers the two little children he has on the flight.

" Where are those two children? Could they have escaped,...?"

"I have to save them too,... because my mummy was very fond of those babies and mummy will be upset if anything happens to them."

But as if he remembered something, his attention turned again to the mummy he saw in the photo.

"Yes,... I've seen this mummy,... this Mummy's hair color,... Yes I still remember,...."

He felt very uncomfortable when he remembered that mummy he saw in that photo again because he can never forget the scenes he saw, it was so disgusting,......

The scenes he had seen so far ran through his mind and the stench around him made him too uncomfortable.

He felt like vomiting but there was nothing left in the stomach to vomit but he was very tired.

His collection of chocolate covers had been more, there was no place left in this bag to collect anymore, and did not have the mind to leave any of it even if it was useless because it was all bought by his mummy for him.

He picked up the covers of chocolates in the bag and began to count them, as if he knew something.

"One, two, three, four,... nine, ten, and so on"

It was then he remembered something he had previously unexpectedly

collected a marker from near a corpse.

He took it in his hands and he felt so curious that he had seen mummy use this many times before. John also had an idea when he saw the part of the white crashed plane.

" Daddy,..... Baby John,...Mummy,..."

" My sweet daddy,...My sweet mummy,... Their sweet baby John,..."

After using the marker he kept it in his little bag without discarding it.

He came back inside the crashed plane and the memories of being on this plane with him and mummy made him smile but before long that smile slowly faded away.

Following the unexpected sound he'd heard from some level of drowsiness. John went back into the woods but he couldn't know that something was trying to impress him out of the darkness of the danger. His mind forbade him not to go, but he ignored it in his eagerness to know.

After a long search following that voice, he finally arrived near the body of the dead woman which he had seen before but by then that strange voice was over.

He looked around in fear because he did not understand anything and only the big trees that were trying to swallow him were in the midst of his helplessness.

All around him was nature waiting patiently, as if to enjoy the danger that lay ahead for John.

Soon, he realized one thing that he had forgotten the way out too.

But at that moment he unexpectedly began to hear again the terrible sound which he had forgotten just before. Now that he understood where the sound had come from, he turned to look at the corpse in fear but suddenly the dead hand of the dead body clung to his feet and pulled him away.

Mummy,... Help me,...

He awoke from his slumber and wiped away the tears.

The relief that all this was just a dream did not last long in him because he could still hear the sound he had heard from his sleep, the same frightening moan.

He was sure there was a creature behind him and that creature might not have been able to see him because he was under the cover of the broken part of the plane.

The light has disappeared and the darkness has begun to appear, it was a frightening sight to see nature set aside for John in the darkness.

He peeked to see what it was with eyes full of fear. That sight was very frightening and his eyes began to fill up. He was very kind to that businessman who had seen on the flight. John now has the wish to save him but knows that it can never be.... Even if saved, there is no significance in it.

A monstrous creature big, blacked, and full of haired something unknown to him is hiding into the woods with dragging the dead body too.

He was only able to stand motionless seeing very pathetic guilt that couldn't help.

Soon the frightening sound and the horrible sight disappeared from his eyes forever into the woods. As if his lost energy had returned to him, he grabbed his bag and ran away and there was very little light left in the sky as if it were just for him.

Doubts have heaped speed for his race as to whether that terrorized creature itself was pursuing.

None of the obstacles he had seen before had now paralyzed him, overcoming all the places where he had fallen before, he sped forward and finally crossed the river.

His legs were slippery from time to time but he was not afraid because he believed that it was better to die than to fall into the hands of the cruel beasts.

He was so tired that he ran so fast, stopped and looked back, and made sure there was no creature behind him.

He still has some left to overcome but it's just muddy places. Seeing those muddy places, he walked towards the water again as if he understood something.

He took off his shoes and washed them in pure water because mummy will be upset if the new shoes get dirty and he held it in his hand and tried to cross the muddy part.

He laid his bare feet on the mud and felt an indescribable discomfort, the wound on his legs dripping with the mud and being bitten by something.

Despite the pain, he refused to wear the shoes on his feet because he could not bear to see his mummy worried.

There was almost knee-deep mud and knee-high pants, so the dress didn't get muddy or it didn't matter because there was no place left in the dress to keep from getting muddy anymore.

A rejoice came and touched his mind with a vain belief that the creature could no longer catch me and by then darkness had completely covered the forest.

"Which way do I go,....?"

The question that arose from him ever shook the atmosphere, it was as if the forest wanted to tell him something, but since he was a small child, the forest must have felt a little affectionate towards him as well.

He had also figured out the way back before he left in the morning, but now he doesn't even know where to go, because everything is covered with darkness and he cannot see anything anymore.

Soon he smelled an accident because he saw the bushes hidden by the darkness behind him, shivering unexpectedly.

It is only after nightfall that the wild animals go out to hunt, and if so, once it comes to this riverbank,...

His voice faltered and tears flowed from his frightened and inanimate eyes.

After waiting for a long time, a small light reflected off the river and entered the forest.

He was very happy with this unexpected change because that light was enough for him to escape.

It was not long before a plant in the wood he noticed in the dim light. Previously, his hand was stained because of that plant and reached his destination based on that particular plant, an indescribable relief passed through his mind.

At last, he approached that fallen old tree and said, with a smile,

"Hai" looking at the tree in a friendly manner again.

In a very short time, John began to feel close to that fallen tree and he decided to take a rest near the root of the fallen tree.

The shoes were holding in his hand were kept securely near the fallen tree and searched for chocolates from his bag.

But the sight bothered him so much that there were very few chocolates left in the bag, even so, he did not forget to leave the rest to mummy and the chocolate was so low that he ate only a few to quench his intense hunger.

He wants to be sedated and doesn't fall asleep and his mind does not calm down.

His mind raced through the experience he had today, so it denied him sleep.

The horrible moments and the horrible things he had seen today came out of his mind without him wanting to, although he was not terrified at the time because of the corpses he saw during the day, his memories of it now haunted him most at night.

"If any of the corpses I saw today came before me now,..?
"

That one condition would be beyond his imagination and he can't even think, it is at night that one is more afraid than during the day because, the light hides nothing but the darkness hides everything and even that corpse too.

He longed for the good sounds of the night so as not to get the thought that I was not alone here.

The silence around him and the darkness of the night frightened him a lot but he began to speak to the nearby fallen tree in a low voice to allay his fear,

" You are my best friend, I hope you know I am sad that I did not see my mummy and in the meantime, you were the only one who comforted me a little....You're so much better than that river that I saw today because I tried to establish a good relationship with that river today but..... he pushed me and injured my forehead."

With horseradish, he made sure there was no blood on his forehead and he continued....

" I will not try to join the river anymore... You pushed me in the morning too but

I didn't get any injuries and....I'm all alone... Will you join me,...?"

He asked, looking at the fallen tree pitifully with horseradish.

As he gazed at the fallen tree,... An idea arose for him,

"Yes,... Idea,..... "

But sleep did not bless him. He is terrified at night because the darkness that pierces his eyes is so frightening to him, when he was at home he was scared to even go to the next room without mummy, but now....

"Because, when I am close to Mummy I'm not myself, I only think about

mummy and I do not think about myself."

Thoughts rising from his mind made him refuse to go to sleep.

The sound of the gushing river could be heard all over the area and that alone is a small relief to him now, but he was very afraid of it because the savage creatures could visit here at any time.

"Won't the wild beasts kill me when they see me,...?"

"There was no need to be so afraid of the teachers at the school, but I was scared and they would not hit me once

I did all my study activities or if they hit me, they would forgive me if I cried.

But even if I cry in front of these creatures, they will kill me because they do not feel sympathy for anything and they only know cruelty. The little animals that hunted and killed all these must have cried like me, not wanting to die....."

After a long sigh, he looked again at the fallen tree that seemed to be his only friend in this forest and made plans in his little mind about something.

"Yes,... Anyway, I have to start that work tomorrow morning," he made the decision.

He was so close to the river, that the bitter cold around made him very restless and he could not sleep.

But no matter how hard he tried, even though he continued his try, quickly his attention shifted to something while trying to fall asleep, his fingers are now under the dry leaves and he feels a little hot.

Soon he gathered the surrounding dry leaves over his body like a blanket.

"I feel an itch but it doesn't matter because the cold has gone away "

He resumed his efforts....

He was as calm as sleep could bless him and he could now clearly hear the sounds around him while going down to the depths for sleep... He heard some of the sounds he had forgotten and in a very low voice in his ears, overcoming the sound of the river from somewhere around him.

Even though he was half asleep, his mind whispered,

"This is not a sound from the forest anyway, If it were, I would have understood from what I had heard for so long and these are the sounds that are familiar to me but I can't understand them. "

He opened his eyes vigorously from the shackles of his sleep. The desire to know arose in him, he stood up and tapped the dry leaves that were spread over him like a blanket.

He can see a little light even when it is very dark all around and he slowly puts his footsteps in the direction of hearing familiar sounds.

Following those sounds he climbed into a bush and entered the forest, clearing the bushes that were obstructing his view.

Finally, he can see the wreckage of the plane across the river now through the bushes in the distance.

But because he is so small, nothing is clear.

John raised his head as he stepped to the towering roots of the nearby tree.

He could see small flickering lights in the distance but he kept trying to see it clearly.

Now he is very close to the river, only the strong sound of the river can be heard and no sound is heard from that distance now.

"Oh that's where I went today, Was there a way out of this too,..? I just went with the other side and fell. It was enough to go through this."

The snow over the river was also a challenge to his clear vision, however, John was not ready to give up.

Without any warning, he unexpectedly heard a loud frightening noise behind him in the silence and suddenly he turned back in shock.

But, what he saw was as if it had given him a new lease of life, A bird like something flying away snatching away a huge snake that was just above him, he could not move until the frightening sound went away from his ear.

He realized with fear that if the bird had been late for a moment, the snake would have climbed into the heights picking him up too.....

Although he had been lost to life by the kind of sight he had seen just before, the realization that he was standing in a very dangerous place gave him a new lease of life.

Although he cannot remember the ways in which he came, through some of the paths he saw in front of him, he somehow managed to get close to the fallen tree.

Now he can see the fallen tree in the distance and he can now be seen only by the dim light reflected from the river but the place where he puts his feet is muddy because it is dark and he cannot see the ways clearly, so he walks ahead realizing that he is likely to fall at any moment.

John turned away from the river and walked along the paths he had walked before, but as soon as he remembered something and moved away from the path and tried to choose another path because he was constantly going in two ways, both of which led him to make mistakes, either he would fall into the mud pit or the stain of the plant would stick to his body, so this time he found a new way to get to the fallen tree.

The new way he had just discovered was safer than the other two ways.

John pays special attention to his experience that the mistakes and failures of his past that are now motivating him to overcome them all,

So face the mistakes and failures with courage, only then can overcome them all.

Soon he returned to the same place where he had been before and then gathered the surrounding dry leaves over his body like a blanket.

The rays of light coming through the branches of the tree hurt his eyes a little, but he can't open his eyes completely and closes them from time to time.

However, he did not want to wake up and worked hard to regain his lost sleep, but sleep was far away from him because the severity of his hunger did not allow him to sleep.

He searched for chocolate in the bag that had been kept aside on one side but found nothing.

Suddenly he remembered one thing, the chocolate was already finished but he had forgotten that it was finished and soon his eyes were slightly wet.

He stared at the chocolate he had set aside for mummy.

"No,... I will not eat this. I set it aside for my mummy..."As if his voice stumbled slightly.

But his decision did not last long. Over time, the severity of his hunger became beyond his control.

There was nothing left in the bag to satisfy his hunger, except the chocolates set aside for mummy. Meanwhile, hunger was forcing him so much but he ignored it and walked to the river bank.

He cemented his position on top of a rock by the river and looked around, from time to time his eyes also turned to the chocolate that was set aside for the mummy.

Reluctantly, he took one of them and put it in his mouth.

When he ate it he felt like he was eating his mummy because his mind was so tired and he knew that this was the only basis of his life before.

After a while, he was able to quench his hunger but could not calm his eyes.

He noticed that his tears were falling and mixing with the river before it gets disappeared.

Meanwhile, a fish frightened him and hid in a small rock then it disappeared from his view. That's when he remembered some of the things he had planned many days ago, then without wanting to waste much more time he ran closer to the fallen tree.

He chose the part of the tree with the roots of the fallen tree because that part was covered with thick roots and soil, and the other part would open.

"That is the door of my house"

He walked to the door of the tree with a small piece of twig lying on the ground and for that moment he remembered his old Mickey.

It seems that it has been exposed to the sun and rain for a long time and the strength of the heartwood and sapwood inside it is very low, so it was easy to stir up. That is why he easily stirred it with a piece of that twig.

The dust was blowing against his face when he stirred but it did not deter him because the goal was to build a whole new house in front of him.

Taking some rest from time to time he resumed his work and finally, he finished his work very nicely and he threw the dust and debris from the stabbing through the main door.

"It is my only one room,...." He said, wiping away the drop of sweat running down his forehead.

He came out of the fallen tree and collected more leaves he had seen around him and stuffed those inside like a bed, then just lay on the top of it,

"Wow.... amazing..... Really like the bed in my real house,....."

The joy of having a new bedroom for him rippled through his face but he was annoyed by the rays of sunshine sneaking into him from the outside.

When he saw this, he remembered that plant which had an adhesive stain.

Soon he ran to that plant and broke its branch and collected the stain that oozed from the broken branch.

At first, he tried to graft with dry leaves, but it didn't work. So he was not disappointed and collected the leaves from nearby plants and grafted them together.

Now it is sticking so at the end of his continuous effort he closed the almost cracks of that fallen tree with the leaves.

But he had a big problem ahead of him because he has to close this door

somehow because he doesn't know if any creatures are coming in,So he thought about it.

One thing caught his attention while looking around, he noticed a thin but big bark of a tree lying outside.

As he walked towards it and thought of something, he made a hole in the middle of it and a nearby wild vine was inserted into the hole and then a piece of a small stick was tied to that end of the wild vine.

He took it and put it on the entryway of the fallen tree and the other end of the wild vine was loaded through the hole above the fallen tree and then tried there with a small piece of twing.

"Yes ...it's not going down anymore... and if ... if I ever need to go out, I just need to untie rope..."John gave himself instruction.

John came out, he was still hungry.

The atmosphere has changed so much that he has been immersed in the work for so long that he could not understand any of the changes around him.

His mind was overjoyed as he looked at his own house that he had built through his hard work.

But by then he was very tired and

Worryingly he took one of the chocolates that had been kept for giving to mummy for so long.

The memories of his mummy fading from his mind came haunting him again and many more questions.

CHAPTER TEN

Recently he has been enjoying walking through the woods very much and soon John has adapted to the very terrible forest though, he is only afraid of his surroundings at night but most of the night time he is asleep so even there he could not understand the real face of surroundings exactly.

He collected a lot of food from the big packet he had kept in his new house and stuffed them in his small bag so he didn't feel too hungry because eating too little food is enough to fill his small hungry stomach.

It was still a good morning for him today. The desire to rush into his mind as usual when he woke up made him wake up from sweet sleep as if his mummy had woken him up before.

"I want to see my mummy,....."

John sobbed from some surface of sleep without him realizing it. His sleepy eyes were slightly scarred, and he opened up, he was still in his own house, but there was only one lack of his mummy.

"If my mummy had been around too, I would have given this big part of myself to my mummy," he said, pointing to one part of his room.

He stepped out of his house and looked closely at the surroundings, realizing that the time was far more out of time now than ever before.

He filled his little bag with packages from the food he had stored.

Thought of something suddenly hit his mind and ran to the river, and empty bottles in his hand were submerged in water and filled with water...

It made him very uncomfortable that memories were constantly calling him from afar.

Memories of being erased lingered in him again, but he did not want to stand still.

"I want to see Mummy,..." John said goodbye to the river and hid in the woods.

John slowed down at a particular sight as he advanced, and he wanted to get closer to it by knocking out the wild vines that stood as if they touched on the earth.

"It was a cave,"

In the stories that someone had told him, he had mostly heard about caves and the treasure that was hidden in the cave and there's a secret behind hiding treasure inside the cave because if it's there, no one can snatch it away.

But he did not see the cave and did not see the treasure, so he knew both of these things that he did not know. Anyway he has seen the cave but he does not know much about the treasure.

He was also very curious about the words that aroused the fact that the treasure was very precious, that it was too beautiful to look at, and that it would shine so beautifully even in the dark.

So it didn't take long for him to develop a strong desire to see the treasure at least once.

"The treasure,...How would it look,.....? Will it shine,.....? I want to see it....."

John prepared to move forward, but he didn't want to back down from his desperate goal and those moments left him with a great deal of conflict.

He also has a keen desire to see the treasure at the same time, even though his favorite and most precious thing is only his own mummy.

"It doesn't matter anyway, after finding the treasure as soon as possible, I'll go looking for mummy because I've come close to the treasure now, but I haven't even reached mummy yet."

He stepped into the cave. It was dark inside the cave, and he was slightly frightened by the sound of bats flapping their wings in the silent cavern as if they had been afraid of hearing his faint footsteps, but he did not back down because all these conditions were now not the first time in his life, but only the experiences he had experienced for so long.

On the way, he remembered something very quickly and began to run back, and soon the light from outside of the cave guided him.

He ran out because it was dark inside, but not because he was afraid of the dark because he could not see any way to go because of the harshness of the darkness.

But he was not prepared to take his thoughts out of the treasure because of any of these obstacles.

John is in the car with mummy right now, and they can't move forward because it's so much of a traffic block. John and Mummy are crowded with vehicles, big and small, unable to move forward.

The sound of the vehicles and the long wait made mummy very uncomfortable. But none of this bothered John very much, John was watching the vehicles around him and the crowds of people from inside the car.

John didn't waste much time, he looked out of the car with his head held high, and by chance, he saw a man, and the thing that attracted him the most from that person was that he was walking very differently from ordinary people, groping with a big stick and walking forward.

Immediately he presented his doubts to his mummy.

"Why was he doing that,....?"

"Oh.... Is that it...? That person can't see... He's a blind man... So when he walks with a stick, he can accurately understand the paths he has to walk, or he uses it to understand if there are any obstacles anywhere in front of him and to find a safer way."

"In that case, I'm facing the same situation now, isn't it?"

He tried to ask mummy in his frenzy, but it moistened his eyes a little as she

wasn't around to answer it.

He knew clearly that there was no point in staying here any longer, and he took the long stick he saw in front of him and disappeared into the cavern, into the darkness.

Though his eyes are open, he sees nothing, only darkness all around him.

He stepped forward with his faltering legs, and the only consolation he was now was the stick in his hand, but while walking he was struck by small boulders and suffered scratches and minor bruises on his legs.

Perhaps it was because he had come a long way through the darkness that he could understand the structure of the darkness, so that even in the dark his eyes could capture certain things and as well as the winged sounds of bats flying as if to snatch him away, all this was frightening him, even in a small way.

Even as he walked forward, he would occasionally look back at his back.

"Should I go back?"

Even though the question was in him, his desires compelled him.

The unexpected sounds and the experiences he feels only because he's in the dark have frightened him so much, yet he's only got a small belief that mummy is with me and I'll never be alone.

His stomach also prevented him from walking too much inside, which smelled unbearable.

Groping in the dark, he took his place somewhere and opened the bag, began to eat chocolates very greedily, and took the water kept in the bag and drank it. He tried to rest for a while, but he couldn't.

The biggest blunder he makes is trying to calm himself down, because he can now clearly hear many voices hidden in the dark, much of which he has not yet heard, and so many frightening thoughts are passing through his mind.

Very upset with everything, John decided to move on.

As he moves forward he stumbles and falls in many places and with the stick in his hand he can only understand distant obstacles but he does not know the very near obstacles.

What he finds more difficult than

obstacles far away are small obstacles that are very close to him.

Before long he fell down after hitting a small obstacle near him. He was sure that he had suffered a severe injury to his knee because he could sense the severe pain and had scratches on several parts of his leg.

To know if there were any wounds, he would immediately rub the painful area with his hands, then taste it from where he felt slightly wet, but it would have the taste of blood, which means that the wounds have been inflicted there.

In any case, even if his condition was very bad, he decided to move forward because this was not his beginning.

The drops of blood flowing through his legs made him very uncomfortable but he didn't cry because he knew very well that no one was going to see his tears, not even him too.

But in parallel with moving forward, mistakes are on the rise.

He had understood the obstacles below and had forgotten to understand the obstacles above his head as he proceeded.

Soon his head pounded hard against something in front of him, and that's when he realized that, "There's no way forward," and no matter how hard he tried, all the way forward was hidden from him.

"Where is the treasure,...?"

"I knew in advance that all this would be a lie, and it would have been enough to go looking for mummy at this lost time."

John yells angrily as if he is telling someone even though he knows there is no one around him, Yet he has no answer and can only hear his voice reflecting back inside the cave.

There may still be very narrow paths left, but the light is so much needed to advance through it that without it he will never be able to escape once he is trapped somewhere.

"I have seen many times before in the videos about the people who climb the cave and the people who work there, I always noticed that there was light in their hands but it was the only thing I did not have in my hand so it is not advisable to go ahead" John told himself.

Anyway, John is sure of one thing that he has come a long way, so he's feeling tired and John is very upset because of the injuries on his head.

He couldn't move very far, and from the shadow of the silence he could hear some groaning and could feel something very close to him, but because it was dark all around him, and could see nothing in front of him and behind.

He was still able to ignore fear because he heard the same voice constantly. Before long he was dragged into a little stupor by the harshness of the darkness.

But, John woke up in a daze because of something unbearable, and then he remembered the wounds he had suffered with a shock.

Something bites and scratches at the wounds, and he picks them up and throws them away, but sooner or later he realizes that they are multiplying uncontrollably, perhaps even more attracted by the taste of his blood ...

Even creatures much smaller than him are chasing and attacking him without any mercy because John is now just a victim in front of them.

Unbeknownst to him, there are other cruels waiting for a good chance to be brutally tortured him under the cover of that darkness, and it is none other than his memories that pervade his realms of thought.

Unable to bear the increasing nuisance, John got up from there and ran away without knowing where to go, but again and again, there was only stupidity in his efforts.

That stick was the only relief to him on his journey through the darkness but he forgot to take it while he was running frantically, and all that was left in his mind was the memory of the moments when he was out, and all that was left in him was the desire to get out somehow.

The intensity of the mistakes he had made was haunting him the most now, and he was beginning to feel a little relieved from fear because he didn't feel too difficult at the place where he was now standing.

" I want to see mummy somehow, it's not safe to stay here for too long, get out as soon as possible,..." A variety of goals disturbed his mind but he was not sure how all this would happen in the dark.

But he took off his legs to walk forward and that too ended up in an accident. Struck by some obstacle in front of him, he broke the same silence that had so loudly dominated the place for a short moment with a terrifying voice.

Yes... He had fallen......Unable to get up......Without trying to get up..... the hint of danger which he had thought in vain that he had broken away before too late began to be reflected in that darkness again.

Yes, they are close enough to attack him again, expecting the taste of his hot blood... He felt as if even that area was shaking because of their abundance.

Anyway, there is no more time to wait and he realizes that his moments are very close.

The time is very close and life is over here and no more story is going to be left here. He finally dissolved into the deep darkness and closed his eyes.

Daddy... Mummy...baby John. Yes, the most beautiful moments he experienced in his life,.... It all ends here.

Are those beautiful moments ending here?

"It could be,...."

The tears that began to flow from his eyes dissolved forever with the soil sometimes indicating his end, but in reality, it was not John's end but, **It was really his beginning.....**

The tears dissolved into the soil and disappeared, but the fragrance remained all over the place, even if only in a small way. It was also his last way of escaping, even if it was something he didn't like.

Everything was so fast that his eyes were opened as he plunged into the darkness, and his longing for the life that was beginning to be lost quickly returned to him.

John searched the water bottle from inside the bag as if he had fixed something in his mind for the last time, and luckily there was full water in it. He immediately poured the water from both bottles onto the ground, made mud from it, and smeared his whole body.

But by then he had been approached by a group of savages who were hiding in the dark and trying to attack him.

They covered him, their weights that couldn't be bearable compared to John, perhaps it was because the scent of blood was not left in him that none of them could recognize him, for the last task of escaping in the panic before death had been done very precisely.

He opened his eyes, covered with mud, which is a sign of his rise, but there are still the savages out there looking for their prey, who have not gone anywhere and are searching with great difficulty in the dark for their own victim.

John laid down without giving even a bit of sound to the savages.

But unexpectedly something had discovered a big cut on his knee.

With a shock, John recognized it and immediately rolled it up in his hands, before it could summon the others.

But the face of extreme cruelty did not hide before John for long, and he squeezed it in his hands and said,

"Yes, all they need is blood, scented hot blood,...I can give you enough of it now."

Even as he kept saying it, his charming smile suggests the brutality lurking at the bottom of his mind.

Even in that little mind, it seems that another face of cruelty is left with it, and John felt no compassion even in the cry of its helplessness for life. He brought it to his mouth and bit it on the neck, as if to inflict a fatal wound... Without any disgust, he tore its body apart greedily and threw away the body of the blood-soaked beast.

Its painful cry for life was only a guide to others who were hidden, before long,he heard a loud sound in his ears from all around him.

Even from the darkness, he could see that countless herds had approached it, With the enthusiasm with which they found their victim,...It's nothing for such a large group, not even he...

This is his way of escape, quickly he took the bag and bottles hidden from him in the dark and walked against the crowd that began to multiply in the darkness.

Even then their swarming was not over, and they quickly hit his legs and were trying to get closer to the victim but the victim's cries had already ended.

He walked with the relief of having escaped death, against the fleeing mobs. His present relief is the cruel darkness that had gathered to kill him in the darkness.

But John could not walk over the rocks as hard as he used to and his legs were stumbling, he couldn't even save his old wounds because of the darkness and did not know the way out but John continued to walk forward not resting anywhere.

Because if he rests in his present state it will surely be the end of him forever, but the condition of his body became so severe that he unknowingly fell there, unable to move forward because John was still only a small child.

CHAPTER ELEVEN

Suddenly he jumped out of his trance as if something was wrapped around his legs but he could not see anything because it was dark all around.

But there was nothing in particular, as he thought in his fear, and he immediately tasted something flowing from somewhere, **'it was water'**

But he was probably shocked by a leaf because he could smell it earlier. He pulled it away and waited there to rest again.

Now he felt a little relief in his mind that if those creatures came to attack him anymore, the mud here would be enough for him.

But he did not even know his eyes were drawn to the object he had just thrown away, but he did not see it because all was dark around.

"Uh yes... I'm sure it'll be a leaf... Where will the big trees remain inside the cave,...? Or if there were any trees, I should have known on the way and...

Where does this water come from,...? "

An answerless to questions affected his composure and become very anxious, the answer to the question lies hidden around him but he had already challenged the darkness.

"Yes.... I'm sure this water is flowing from outside because there are trees and plants outside the cave."

Then he looked at nothing else, he walked against the oozing water.

From time to time his legs slipped and sank into the mud because it was dark and it was all hidden from him.

He had no idea of the way forward because he had forgotten the stick somewhere, but he was still firm in his faith.

As he walked forward, he realized one thing in the strengthening of the flow of water, 'The well-flowing indicates the depth, that is, he is now approaching a very deep place somewhere in this cave, and not only that, but due to the force of the flow, the chances of his feet slipping and falling on top of the boulders are much higher than before.'

But time was still not up to the mark, and as he could understand the low flow area, he immediately shifted his steps and focused on the less flowing side.

His hard work, which lasted for a long time, did not tire him out. The joy of finding a way out had prompted him to break through the obstacles ahead and move forward.

Soon the light that had departed from the outside long ago kissed his eyes as if by love.... In his mind the rays of joy and gladness and the rays of light had intertwined.

Seeing the light, his speed faster than usual, would a higher speed put him in danger again,....?

In the meantime, he had reached the cavern.

But it was raining well outside, and after thinking about something, he dissolved into the rain because it was this rain that saved him from the big danger he was trapped in.

Mummy's advice not to play in the rain didn't bother him and it was as if his lost smile was attached to him again...The little boy's joy must have been looking around innocently but he had not deliberately paid any attention to it.

Time has crossed boundaries, and the darkness is patiently waiting for the light around it to become just a memory. Perhaps that is why the poor animals have begun to lose the freedom and joy they had when there was light, and that is why they are trying to close their eyes to silence because now they have to watch with fear and guard their ways because it is the turn of the savages to try to hunt in hiding.

Soon a vibration began to sound across the forest, there could hear the sound of birds rising out of the silence as if frightened by the sound of something.

The sound of someone running at high speed, pressing the dry leaves through the bushes, It was none other than John.

He's afraid of the dark like the rest of the poor animals and he's struggling to run as fast as he can to his home in the woods, Because he, like the rest of the creatures and he is one of the poor creatures in that big forest.

John had now begun to learn more or less about the ways of the forest, so he was able to get closer to his abode earlier than usual.

But what he saw made his eyes moisten for a moment.

His house was almost covered with fallen leaves, and the beauty of his house, which had been when it was built, has now diminished considerably,

but he doesn't have to be too worried about it, because there's only a problem that ends up being cleaned up.

But John does not have time and strength to clean up there now because the atmosphere is already addicted to darkness, and John is very restless and tired because of his wounds.

A small sigh of something unexpectedly rang in his ears, and John overcame the knots of his sleep and opened his eyes.

But everything is the same as before, he can not see anything in particular because there is only darkness around. But its voice was enough to make John realize what was hidden.

"Like something is dragging....Perhaps it's a snake."

He also has in his mind a memory that influences his conjecture.

That is, earlier John would regularly pile fallen leaves over his body and take shelter from the cold.

Now that he's so close to the river, he's had to deal with the cold of the night before, and the snake must have been trying for warmth among the dry leaves, but this is an extreme danger compared to John because, his mummy always refused to let him out into the woods outside the house.

The only word Mummy always said was still in his mind, "Don't go there... There will be snakes sometimes."

"Snake.... Isn't that a small animal,...? Then why should I be afraid of it.....?"

"No John.... Never.... snakes are very dangerous creatures because the deadly venom inside them can kill even a big monster. But my sweetie need not be afraid, if you have Mummy with you it will never hurt you....."

"I don't have a mummy with me now. Will it hurt then,....?" After a short pause, John continued, "After all, I have to start my work tomorrow morning, sweep away all the fallen leaves around my house, so that the snakes won't get warm from here."

John opened his eyes again as if forcibly, out of some depth of drowsiness.

"Is it morning,.....?"

The sounds of the birds heard from outside the fallen tree must be the answer to his question.

John was feeling very thirsty, and immediately he opened the bag and searched for the water bottle, but found it in the bag, but there was not a drop of water left in it.

John soon came out of his house and ran towards a nearby river.

Reaching the river bank, he is now fully aware of every hidden danger.

With the help of the rocks near the river, he discovered the place where the pure water flowed and immersed his bottle in it. Although the bottle was rising because of the force of the water, John applied enough force against the water and collected enough water because this was not the first experience of his life.

The water in the filled bottle was raised to bring it closer to his mouth, and the unexpected sight of something thwarted his attempt.

The wreckage of the crashed plane is nowhere to be seen, it's empty there. His mind was filled with doubts about it, but he flew them all away in the passing breeze because many of his questions had been left unanswered by this huge forest.

This suspicion, which John now feels, is only one of them.

The wreckage of the flight and dead bodies he had forgotten flashed through his mind again and even now he still did not believe it was his mummy, there was no doubt left because, "MY MUMMY WOULD NOT DIE..." Again and again, he kept repeating the same words.

His last moments with his mummy passed through his mind and he was unknowingly seeping tears strcaming down his eyes also the guilt that this was all because of him broke his mind.

"I should never have disobeyed mummy. Maybe it's because I showed it that's what happened to me now."

He was drawn to a memory of something and he closed his eyes with extreme guilt.

"John, you get up now fast.... It is time to go see daddy, hurry... "

"No Mummy I need to sleep...I am not coming".

He lay there, not wanting to wake up from his sleep.

Mummy heard his reply and went back without disturbing him because mummy knows his character very well and if he does not like something he will keep crying, so he thought from some depth of sleep that mummy would not bother him anymore.

But things did not turn out as he hoped. He got up because he knew that cold water was falling on him, opened his eyes and saw that he was lying in the bathtub as well as mummy pouring cold water on his body.

"I will never talk to my mummy again"

John said very helplessly.

"Okay it doesn't matter, I know you will come to me again"

Mummy's sarcastic words hurt him a lot and also she scolded him for being reluctant to take a bath.

He could not bear any of this at all and he decided that he would never be quiet with his mummy...

While bathing him, Mummy ran to the next room as if remembering something because mummy forgot to take the bath towel.

A lot of thoughts went through his mind at the same time as the mummy disappeared from sight.

John could not control his anger and sadness because of his mummy waking him up in the early morning and also the mummy's atrocities.

"This is the perfect time for me to take revenge on my mummy," He decided.

John quickly got out of the bathtub and closed the bathroom door and locked it.

Then he walked back to the bathtub and sat after draining the water from the bathtub.

Then, after a while, John opened his eyes to the sound of his mummy knocking on the door.

Soon he woke up in fear when he heard the mummy's loud yell, but by then time had gone too far.

Suddenly he ran to the door in the bathroom but didn't have the courage to open it because he was sure that mummy would hit him anyway once he opened it. But because of his mummy's insistence, he had no choice but to do so.

At last, he opened the door with horseradish eyes.

His mummy's helpless face outside the door disappointed him a lot.

"I am so.sorry... I didn't know ....because of my anger...."

He does not know what to say to look at that mummy's face.

But mummy didn't do anything to him as he expected and the smile still didn't fade on his mummy's face.

"Yes... Now I can understand because of me, we missed the flight we were supposed to take and that's why mummy decided to come on this flight... and that is what all wrong happened to my life." His mind blamed him.

It is too late. Only the darkness that closes them all around.

He remembered the path in the forest but could do nothing because all around was dark.

He is resting under a tree because it is night, when it is the night he will try to fall asleep quickly because he knows that, it is so scary to see the horrible moment of the night.

It was then that he saw a sight very unexpectedly, a woman was walking somewhere in the darkness of the forest.

The belief that someone was still alive in the forest made him very happy.

He very much wanted to see that woman and quickly ran after the woman.

"Hello... will you save me,...? I am stuck in this jungle... and I want to see my mummy,"

He said aloud but the woman did not look back and hurried to walk.

However, he is not ready to give up on that attempt because it is his wish to escape too.

He also quickly followed that woman but she is running somewhere in the woods fastly, John has called her very loudly but she doesn't hear.

Unexpectedly, the woman disappeared from his sight, John looked around for the woman but could not find her.

At last, he saw the woman standing a short distance in front of him but he couldn't see her face because she turned back and he slowly got closer to her.

"Hello... Madam.... Have you seen my mummy,...?"

When she heard this question, she quickly turned to him, suddenly he was scared because the woman had a half-burned face and also... **'It was his own Mummy......'**

He broke his sleeping curtain and got up and realized it was just a dream but now John was really shocked, his own mummy standing in front of him as he saw in his scary dream.

But somehow he understood that he saw both of these only from a dream because now there is no one in front of him and he is lying just near the fallen tree.

He was afraid to see his mummy in his sleep but now he wanted to, yes,... He wanted to see his old mummy, "My so pretty mummy"

" How did I get out of the tree,..?"

That's when he realized something was wrong.

"I was supposed to rest here for a while yesterday but fell asleep unknowingly.

Although he had no desire to go near the river, he walked towards the river that night.

The light of the moon reflected from the river was a comfort to him and he looked up from the riverbank to the place where the wreckage of the plane was left but heavy snow covered it completely and the light of the moon shone on the snow and reflected like a diamond.

He was so disappointed and he sat down on the rock.

"I think it is because of me... If we had gone on the first flight then there would not have been such a fate now...If I had just obeyed my Mummy's words,....I would be living happily with my daddy and mummy today...."

"Could my mummy have died like them because of the mistake I made,...?"

An unexpected question arose from the bottom of his mind but he can never bear this question anymore.

"If my mummy dies, I will surely die and

I cannot live without my mummy...**No..... my mummy will never die,..** One day I will see my mummy anyway...."

Unbeknownst to him his voice was rising all over the place but it was time for the cruel creatures to open their eyes shining in the dark.

His guilt will never comfort him but will only put him in more danger.

He understood the signs of nightfall with fear but he didn't want to leave, because the unanswered questions had paralyzed him.

He sat there looking at the flowing river with flowing tears, the light of the moon reflected on the tears and flashed into his eyes.

He looked up at the sky and saw that the moon was shining there and the moon is the only reason why all shines even in the dark.

Rapidly, his eyes filled because he has been seeing the moon for a long time now.

He still remembers... When was the last time he saw the moon in the sky...

That was also a night, but that was the last night of his life, the last night he was with his mummy.

"Mummy was with me that day but..... That was the last ever...."

The overflowing tears made him very uncomfortable but he could not wipe it away,he was still motionless except for his opened eyes.

Suddenly, the attention went to the dense bushes and he could hear very small sounds and suppressed movements that were unfamiliar.

Soon he realized that those strange footsteps had crossed the puddles and were very close behind him, he did not have the courage to look back and ran fast forward in fear.

While running forward, he confirmed that some creature was coming to attack him from behind because the running footsteps with him were an exact proof of that.

Desiring to escape, he ran to the heart of the forest but he had no idea where he was going, everything around was still unfamiliar to him, even the ferocious beast that came to attack him from behind.

While trying to run forward past a crowded bush, he tapped his foot on the root of the tree and fell down, but he could not get up because his fall was so strong.

One thing he was sure of was that the creature would jump on top of him and kill him soon.... He believed that what he had left of these moments would be a tragic death.

This will definitely happen, only at an unexpected time.

But nothing happened as he expected and he continuously looked back without being able to believe it because nothing was found behind.

The silence enveloped him and surround him, his only relief was the light coming from the sky and over the forest.

The vain belief of " These were just my feelings" no longer followed him, turned back in shock when he heard the unexpected sound of dry leaves being strongly pressed by something from behind.

Seeing that sight, his eyes widened in disbelief.

"Wolf....."

He pursed his lips unknowingly, and watched with horrified eyes as it appeared in front of him under the moonlight.

"THE WHITE WOLF...."

It was the same color as the moon but the strongest he had ever seen. It had been following John so far and was sure it would be the same.

John was frightened when he saw that beast but he did not have the strength to run so, didn't even try to escape because John could see the kindness in its eyes.

It slowly came closer to him, smelling the way he had come.

Even though it was very close to him, John was not scared because he was more skeptical of the fear in him.

In the end, it was very close to him but he did not move, it smelled from his feet to his head and still, John did not move.

After his neck, his lips, his eyes, and finally approached his forehead but he felt very uncomfortable and soon his eyes filled and overflowed.

A memory of something had invaded his mind with lightning speed.

Unable to control himself he forgot the whole area and hugged the wolf's neck because his mind was full of memories of the last time his mummy kissed him before she left, but the wolf did not retaliate in his unexpected behavior and remained there.

In such a short time, John felt very close to that terrifying creature, could that beast have had pity on John, too, ...?

John asked, stroking the wolf's face with his soft little fingers," **Have you seen my mummy,..?"**

But there was no answer from that wolf. It did not disappoint him and after looking at him for a moment it went ahead.

He decided to wait until the wolf he liked so much disappeared from his view.

But,....

That creature suddenly turned back at John without expecting anything at all, and made a cruel sound, quickly running towards him with cruel eyes.

At last, **THE EVIL CREATURE** jumped on him with extreme force, but it was an attack that the baby child could not ever bear.

Suddenly, he fell so hard that his head hit the rock nearby and soon his eyesight began to blur and body became motionless as before.

But, ... He could still enjoy those cruel moments that the darkness set aside for that baby John,.....

IT NEVER GOES AN END, BUT.....

IT WILL CONTINUE......

www.ingramcontent.com/pod-product-compliance
Lightning Source LLC
Chambersburg PA
CBHW051242130726
47988CB00001B/464